Metaphorosis

Jul-Sep 2024

Beautifully made speculative fiction

Also from Metaphorosis

Metaphorosis

Jul-Sep 2024

edited by
B. Morris Allen

ISSN: 2573-136X (online)
ISBN: 978-1-64076-282-4 (e-book)
ISBN: 978-1-64076-283-1 (paperback)

Metaphorosis
a magazine of speculative fiction
from
Metaphorosis Publishing

Neskowin

Jul-Sep 2024

A word about Michael Gardner

Michael Gardner is a member of the elite Meta4osis club — authors who've published four or more stories with us. We didn't accept his first story, but the second became "Renewal", published in September 2017. From then on, we published "This Side of the Wall" in January 2018, at 15,362 words, the longest full story we've ever published; "Nana Naoko's Garden" in October 2018; and "All That Remains", in August 2020.

We like Michael's work so much that he's one of just five authors whose work we've published in serial form, with "Infinite Possibilities" published from September to December 2022.

One of Michael's strengths is an ability to take outlandish situations and not only make them plausible, but show the human and emotional trials of the characters that confront them. The following story, "Colossus", is a perfect example.

Colossus

Michael Gardner

Alexi Vanderbilt lived in the upper right thigh of the Colossus. Floor to ceiling windows built into the flesh of the mummified giant afforded him a handsome view of the ocean. It was angry, and lashed the coast on which the Colossus stood with foam crested waves. On the horizon were dark clouds, lightning spiderwebbing their underbellies. A storm that was predicted to reach landfall before it exhausted itself, something the colonists had no record of.

Alexi had originally found the forecast hard to believe, but the wind had risen violently during the last hour and now rattled the window in its frame. He felt the drop in temperature through the glass. Alexi's days were largely indistinguishable from each other, so the prospect of something new caused his skin to tingle with anticipation.

The apartment system chimed softly. "Show message," Alexi said, his attention still with the storm. There was a gentle clicking sound, then Miriam's message with details of his next job appeared in green text within the glass of the window. It brought him quickly back to mundanity. He sighed, read it. Excessive heat in one of the premium apartments. Mr Rowbotham's residence. He had the vague recollection of doing some work there last year. Maybe the year before. If he recalled correctly, Mr Rowbotham was an elderly man that insisted on being called Commander.

"Remind me of the location," he said. The text dissolved, became an image of the complex and in red, a rectangle showing him a large apartment, top centre in the chest. "Log the job. I'll be up shortly."

The image faded. A gust of wind spattered the outside of the window with fine droplets of rain. It stopped as quickly as it started. Alexi leaned closer to the glass, ran a dirty finger along the window surface, leaving a smudge. He shook his head, smirked. Unbelievable.

After taking a last glance at the storm, he collected his bag of tools from the kitchen bench and left his apartment.

The Commander led Alexi to the kitchen. "You feel that, son? It's like the oven's running."

Alexi frowned, peered over the kitchen bench to confirm there was an oven and it was indeed off. Alexi didn't use an oven. Too old fashioned. And expensive. The Commander's kitchen opened into a spacious loungeroom with expansive windows. They offered panoramic views that took in the ocean, the sprawling terraformed gardens that surrounded the Colossus, and the barren desert beyond. He wondered how the Commander had afforded such a prime location, such a large space. He appraised the man with a sideways glance. Straight back, tall, grey crewcut. "It is warm," Alexi admitted.

The Commander gave a curt nod. Alexi placed his bag of tools on the ground, removed a flex screen, unfolded it. Moving his fingers swiftly across the thin glass, he brought up the diagnostic program, attempted connection to the Commander's home system. He was prompted for approval. He passed the screen to the Commander, who raised it for an eye scan, handed it back.

"The kitchen is running five degrees above your preferred settings. The air conditioning system is attempting to compensate but is failing. The kitchen is the hottest room, but your entire apartment is warmer than average. This is odd. It's possible the storm is interfering with our systems." Alexi glanced across the loungeroom and out the windows to the purple-grey clouds that filled the sky. There were now several columns of hazy rain falling in the distance over the water.

"Huh," the Commander said, an exhalation of breath. "Perhaps. Or perhaps it's age. Some days I feel this complex is degenerating more quickly than me. You should have seen it when it was new."

Alexi looked up from his screen, found the Commander regarding him with sharp eyes. "You were here when this was first built?" Alexi asked.

A smile flickered across the Commander's lips. "I was. I was the first person to move into the Colossus."

"You don't look old enough," Alexi blurted out.

The Commander chuckled, an odd, staccato sound. "Oh, I'm plenty old enough. I'm first-generation. I've had some regenerative work, but the best tip I can give is stay active, physically and mentally."

"I will, sir. Do you mind if I ask what you did?"

"Engineer. I helped build the offshore mining rigs after we landed, but my proudest contribution was solving our permanent accommodation issue. We overcame the lack of natural resources by utilising this," he said, gesturing to the apartment.

Alexi whistled softly. There weren't many first gens left. Alexi found it hard to imagine what it had been like for them. Life seemed so routine now. Dull, even.

In contrast, this man had volunteered for a one-way trip in stasis. Had woken over a decade later to establish the colony and build the laser array to propel the light sails of the fleet that followed. Millions of people had relied on them.

Without the colony's propulsion system, the carriers would never have achieved the speeds necessary to reach the new home world with sufficient fuel and supplies.

The first gens had known they wouldn't follow the fleet. Everything they brought with them was used to construct the mines and laser array, including their ships which were broken down and repurposed. The first gens epitomised sacrifice for the greater good. Their reward was to watch the carriers pass, to celebrate and farewell them with blasts from the array, then to exist as best they could. Yet Alexi sensed pride emanating from the Commander. A sense of purpose and contentment.

What did Alexi have in comparison? He hadn't contributed to the great mission. The salvation of humankind had been achieved long before he was born. The biggest event in his life had been choosing a career of maintenance over mining. Some days, he wondered if it would have made any difference had he simply chosen to sit around all day doing nothing.

He noticed the Commander waiting, watching. "Thank you for your service, sir," Alexi said.

The Commander smiled, nodded. Alexi cleared his throat; conscious he wasn't paid for chit chat. "Do you mind if I check your service hatch?"

"Of course."

The Commander led Alexi from the kitchen into a short hallway. The silver hatch was built into the far end. The Commander unlocked it with an eye scan, and Alexi pulled it open, leant inside, then jerked back like he'd been slapped.

"What's wrong, son?" the Commander asked from just behind.

"The heat," Alexi said. But that wasn't the whole truth. When he'd thrust his head inside the hatch, he'd heard something: a low thump. A sound like a soft strike of a bass drum. He eased his head back inside the hatch, found it silent. He used his flex screen to turn on the dull strip lighting in the hatch. He examined the mummified, grey flesh of the Colossus hidden just behind the apartment walls. It was marbled with fibre and copper cabling, reinforced with steel beams. But something was odd. The flesh, which had always been dry, glistened. He ran fingers along the surface, found it warm, damp. He removed a thin silver probe from his jacket, pierced the flesh, watched readings flicker across his screen.

He read them in disbelief.

He read them again.

"Find anything?" the Commander asked, and Alexi jumped. He took a breath, removed his head from the hatch.

"Maybe. But I need to run further tests." He looked around for his tool bag, realised he'd left it in the kitchen. "I'll just grab my bag." He turned to go, but stopped when the Commander said, "What the hell is that?"

Alexi turned and found the Commander pointing. He followed the outstretched finger toward the thin probe that Alexi had left impaled in the flesh wall. From it ran a thin trickle of something darkly red which looked very much like what it couldn't be. Blood.

"There are five more complaints about excess heat on floors eighty-six, seven and nine. There are also two complaints about noise on floor eighty-three," Miriam said through the transmitter.

"We have a problem, Miriam."

"You're closest to the Armitages', should I alert them that you will attend to them next?"

"Are you listening? We have an issue. Something strange is happening."

A pause. "What do you mean?"

Alexi took a breath. "The heat in Mr Rowbotham's apartment is not a result of faults in the wiring or air conditioning. The heat is being generated by the flesh of the Colossus."

A longer pause. "I don't understand what you're trying to tell me. We have complaints lining up. We need to address them. That is your—"

"I know what my job is," Alexi interrupted. "I'm telling you the heat is not a fault in the system. It's the... it's..."

"What?"

He sighed. Gathered his thoughts. "The inner wall was bleeding."

It was a long time before Miriam spoke. "But that's impossible."

"I'll send you my readings."

"Okay. But while I review them, make yourself useful. Check the central climate control system. Just in case."

Flurries of rain slapped at the windows that lined the corridor. Alexi stopped and pressed his face to the glass, looked down. He saw rain falling for the first time upon the terraformed gardens around the Colossus, and the large desalination plant that supported them. Up to now, rain had seemed a distant phenomenon, something that fell well out over the ocean. He shook his head, set off again toward the access panel. The wind buffeted the apartments.

Alexi unlocked the access panel, pulled it aside, stepped through into the vast space beyond. The sound of the rain grew softer.

The climate control system had been built on the remains of the Colossus' diaphragm. The space in which it sat was cavernous, gloomy. Grey flesh infused with fibre cables, copper, criss-crossed steel beams. Yellowed ribs encased huge lungs that hung loose and deflated like ancient curtains. The room smelled of dry earth.

The huge cavity was poorly lit, so Alexi switched on his torch. He aimed it toward the middle, where the light feathered across the steel housing of the distant climate system. It was large, about the size of one of the smaller apartments in the calves of the Colossus. He stepped carefully across the uneven floor of muscle, began the trek toward the system. The floor felt spongier than he remembered.

When he reached the system, he found the casing covered in moisture. Alexi ran a finger along it, raised the liquid toward his nose, sniffed. It smelled of nothing. Water, he presumed.

He opened the access panel, connected his flex screen, which told him that the system was working overtime to compensate for excess heat throughout the building. Alexi found no faults with the system itself. He disconnected, closed the panel, had turned to go when he heard a loud thump from above. He jumped, swung his torch up, the beam wavering.

He ran the light slowly over ancient, rubbery arteries. The usually deflated white casings were semi-engorged, crimson beneath. He shone the torch on the monstrous grey heart, usually withered. Not now; it had swollen. As he watched, it clenched. Alexi nearly dropped the torch, regathered, tried to hold the beam steady. He saw the heart release and the sound it made was a deep thwomp. The vessels around it shivered, red pulsed, stopped. Everything was still again.

Miriam sat behind her white desk, eyes closed, nose pinched between thumb and forefinger. Her office was immaculately clean, smelt lightly of bleach. There were no decorations on the walls. The only furniture was the desk, the bank of computers, the two black chairs opposite her in which Alexi and the Commander sat. Behind her, glass panes allowed a view of the desert, the corundum mine visible on the horizon.

"That's impossible," she said again.

"I know."

She opened her eyes, let her gaze drift from Alexi to the Commander, who sat ramrod straight. "And why are you here?"

"The Commander was with me when we discovered the blood. He also designed these apartments. I thought he might be of assistance."

Miriam cleared her throat. "Okay. If there is light to shed here, please do, because presently I'm at a loss to know what to do with this information."

Alexi turned and looked hopefully at the Commander. For a beat, all he saw was an old man, but then something hardened in the Commander's eyes.

"I can't explain why the Colossus has begun to regenerate. It's as unfathomable to me as to you, ma'am. But for whatever it's worth, I can provide a little history.

"I was on the first ship of colonists to arrive, and the presence of the giants was a shock. Our scouting crafts and probes had no record of sophisticated lifeforms, and yet we discovered six colossal, sexless bipeds, somewhat reminiscent of huge Neanderthals. This had either been a terrible, improbable miss, or evidence that the giants had been first hidden, then mobile in the years between our initial explorations and the arrival of the mission.

"We were initially very wary. But investigations revealed that the giants were lifeless, even though the corpses exhibited few signs of natural decay. It was like they had been unnaturally preserved; their poses staged."

"Which is impossible?"

"Yes."

"So, if you knew so little about them, why take the risk of utilising them for housing?"

"We were only twelve years ahead of the interstellar fleet and our primary objective was the laser array. The successful settlement of humans on the new world—El-Salalong—depended on an operational array propelling the light sails of the fleet as they sling-shotted around this planet.

"We had sufficient materials to build the array, the corundum mines, and temporary accommodations. Long-term arrangements were left to our ingenuity. But as you can see from that view behind you ma'am, natural building resources were not readily available.

"The giants presented a solution. We had ample sand for glass, we had some iron supplies, but there were no trees, just scrubby bush and seaweed. The giants offered an existing structure that we could utilise for our homes."

"I'm assuming you triple checked they were dead before you moved in?"

The Commander snorted a laugh. "I can absolutely assure you they were. The readings we took suggested they had been dead longer than we knew was possible given previous observations of the planet. The flesh had dried and hardened into something reminiscent of timber, the bones like concrete. The idea that they are now softening, well…"

"Yes, well…"

There was a long silence, which Alexi chose to break first. "What do we do?"

Miriam sighed, closed her eyes again, shook her head. As she opened her mouth to speak there was a groan, the floor of the office jolted hard, and the glass behind Miriam cracked from base to top. The three looked at each other with wide, stunned eyes.

"An earthquake?" Alexi asked.

"I think," the Commander said quietly, "The Colossus just moved."

Alexi stepped out of the giant's foot and into driving rain. The wind gusted strongly, and he had to lean into it. He squinted against the deluge, raised his hand. He was soon drenched, cold. The scent of salt from the ocean overpowered the usual dusty smells of the desert.

Lightning flickered overhead, followed closely by the low rumbling of thunder.

The waves of the sea were white capped peaks, lashing the shore a few hundred metres away. Date trees swayed in the storm, and the shrubs around the Colossus cowered close to the ground, beaten down by the rain.

Behind him, the building moaned. Alexi spun round, looked up and shielded his eyes against the stinging rain. He tried to spy what had caused the sound, tried to check his memory of the creature's longstanding pose. The task seemed impossible. It was difficult to take the creature all in at once, and as he scanned the Colossus from top to bottom, shoulder to shoulder, he realised that for years Alexi had taken its presence for granted. An inert structure, blue tinted windows cut into the flesh. But now, outside, with the image of the creature's beating heart in his mind, he looked upon the form anew. It stood tall, proud, one foot slightly ahead of the other, arm raised and pointed to sea. Yet the grey, dried skin around the glass seemed ruddier. And although he could not sense any significant change in the giant's position, he felt it leered down at him. He shivered.

Another moan. Alexi's eyes darted about, finally settled upon a trickle of broken glass that fell from high up. The glass glinted as it fell, the sound of it striking the sand obscured by the downpour.

He engaged the transmitter in his jacket, called Miriam.

"There's evidence of more damage outside," he yelled over the din of the storm. "There're broken windows, and glass is falling. I'm worried about the structural integrity of the building." And he was worried the Colossus was waking, which was what he refused to say out loud. The thought was equally frightening and exhilarating.

"What do you suggest?"

"Ultimately, it's your call. But I think we should evacuate. Otherwise, we'll find ourselves stuck in this thing."

He heard soft breathing from Miriam. "Do you think it has something to do with the storm? The electrical activity?"

"I don't know. I honestly don't."

"Where would our people go?"

"The mine."

"Let me put in some calls to the other colossi. If they're not exhibiting the same changes, they might offer better options then the mine."

"And if they are?"

"Just let me make the calls. You prepare the vehicles."

Alexi drove the fourth transporter up out of the subterranean car park and onto wet sand when Miriam's voice broke into the cab. "It's not just us," she hissed. "The Warrior has collapsed. The Lady is trying to fucking stand. Some of the apartments have been crushed. They estimate twenty-two colonists dead, more injured."

Alexi sat in the cool cab of the transporter, breathed heavily. "Dead?"

"Dead, Alexi. The giants are coming to life and crushing the inhabitants."

"Why didn't your colleagues warn us?"

"They were pretty fucking busy trying to save themselves."

Alexi felt time slow for a moment, then it snapped back fast. He blinked a couple of times, rubbed his hands furiously over his face to clear his head. "We need to evacuate, Miriam. Now."

"Okay," she said. Alexi heard a siren wail from inside the Colossus. He opened the transporter doors, stepped out into the rain. He looked up, saw more fragments of glass falling to the ground.

He took in the outstretched hand of the Colossus, saw it clenched, not finger extended as it should be. The skin was a deep brown hue. There was new hair on the knuckles, on the forearms, curling over the blue glass in its wrist.

Alexi tore his gaze from the giant, ran into the building.

As the residents emerged from the stairwell Alexi directed them outside and toward the transporters. The residents looked frightened, panicked, so Alexi did his best to maintain calm. But it was difficult with the building—he had to stop thinking that way—the leg of the giant shaking.

The foyer jolted suddenly, the walls cracked loudly, and Alexi stumbled to the floor, plaster showering down upon him. He waited on all fours until the shuddering stopped. Waited a moment more. When all seemed still, he rose, helped a middle-aged man to his feet, ushered him outside onto the wet beach. When he returned to the foyer, he found it empty, but then Miriam appeared on the stairs, her face bleeding, a bruise forming on her temple. She lurched across the foyer, and Alexi grabbed her by the arm, steadied her, looked into wild eyes.

"Everyone except us and the Commander is outside. We need to go."

"Wait. The Commander?"

"I tried, Alexi, but he refused to leave. Muttered something about this being his creation. He said he wanted to see it through to the end."

"We can't leave him. He's an old man."

Miriam broke free of Alexi's grip, stumbled when the foyer rumbled again, but held her feet, as did Alexi. "He's made his fucking choice. We have a responsibility to the rest," she said, then ran outside without looking back.

Alexi watched her go. Just above the sounds of the storm, he heard a transporter roar to life. He took a step toward the exit, stopped. Looked back. He didn't owe anything to the Commander. The last vehicle was outside waiting for him. But the Commander and the rest of the first gens hadn't owed anything to humanity either. And still they had risked their lives for the betterment of those that came behind. The chance for millions to reach a habitable new world, while they remained here on this shitty outpost.

Sacrifice. When had Alexi done anything so meaningful? His life was maintenance. Keeping the status quo. Where was his purpose?

He glanced at the door, the elevators Miriam had shut down for safety, the warped staircase. "Shit," he muttered to himself, then ran toward the stairs.

Alexi stood on the sixty first floor landing, bent over, hands on knees, dry retching. He regained control, sucked in a huge breath, cleared his throat, spat. The saliva hit the cement with a splat. His breath was ragged, his chest burned.

The stairs beneath him groaned, the walls of the stairwell shuddered. With a squeal, the landing beneath him buckled, cracked, then most of it fell away.

As the floor went, he leapt on instinct, grabbed hold of the balustrade still connected to the wall of the stairwell. His body jerked against his grip, nearly loosened his fingers, but he held on grimly, feet dangling over nothing. He refused to look down, but heard the cacophony of the stairs still collapsing. Dust filled the air around him with the acrid scent of cement. He gritted his teeth, pulled, his muscles aching, and slowly eased himself up onto what remained of the broken staircase.

The Colossus shuddered. Alexi gripped the railing tight. When it steadied, he sucked in a breath. Here was that adventure he'd been craving, he thought, grinned. He fought back the urge to laugh manically, began his ascent again.

Breathing hard, Alexi buzzed the doorbell as the building around him shivered. He held on tightly to the door handle to stop himself toppling. As he waited, it hit him that the stairwell was gone, that escape was no longer simple. His stomach constricted painfully; his throat went dry. He swallowed to stop from panicking, forced himself to think.

Several service tunnels linked the upper floors. There might yet be a way to use them to get down to a point where the stairs remained intact. It was worth a try, he thought.

The door swung inward suddenly and Alexi fell with it, lost his grip, and slid across the floor past the Commander, who was pressed hard against the foyer wall. "What are you doing here, son?" the Commander asked, staring at Alexi as he tried to scrabble to his feet. The floor shifted again.

"You need to get out," Alexi said.

"I've already made up my mind. I told Miriam."

"You're fucking crazy. You don't know what you're saying," Alexi screeched, rose, staggered toward the Commander, then fell painfully upon his knees as the apartment lurched.

Alexi swallowed down the hurt, looked up at the Commander. "This fucking thing is alive. We need to go. Now."

"It's incredible, isn't it? I spent my life working on the Colossus, moulding it, reshaping it, living inside it. All the while wondering what it had been like when it was alive. I don't have to wonder anymore, Alexi. I'm going with it. A final adventure."

Alex opened his mouth to argue, but was cut off by an incredible rending sound, so loud that Alexi thought his eardrums would burst. He lifted his hands from the floor to cover his ears, but as soon as he did, he slid again across the floor of the apartment, now tilted alarmingly toward the large windows.

As he careened toward the glass, he saw the view was changing. Instead of storm clouds, he saw roiling waves crashing against the beach. Then he saw the Colossus' foot and ankle buried in the sand.

Alexi smashed hard into the glass, which shuddered in its frame. The jolt knocked the wind from him. He clawed at his neck, tried to force air in. The Commander slammed into the glass beside him a moment later. Spiderwebs of cracks appeared, ran across the surface of the glass. The old man whimpered, went limp.

The Colossus continued to shift. An armchair tumbled across the room and smashed into the window, which groaned and cracked more. The window tilted further, until Alexi found the glass beneath him instead of the floor.

A giant, haired arm encroached on Alexi's view. The arm pushed down with force, the hand speared into the ocean with an explosion of water. The Colossus shuddered, but the arm steadied the giant's fall. The apartment stilled. Air seeped back into Alexi's lungs.

Gingerly, he tried to rise, but as soon as he placed weight on the glass, it moaned, and splintered. He quickly lay back down, distributed his weight, then slid slowly toward the Commander. He shook the old man's shoulder.

"Commander. Wake up."

But the man didn't move. The glass groaned again, a piece the size of a dinner plate breaking away from the corner of the frame. Alexi watched it tumble toward the water, which seemed very far away even with the Colossus bent over. The sounds of the storm intensified. A gust of wind invaded the apartment.

He grabbed the collar of the Commander's shirt, moved away from the middle of the glass, pulled the Commander after him. He made his way slowly toward the edge of the window, wrapped his free hand around the window frame where the glass had broken away.

The apartment shook again, the Colossus began to rise, the view shifting up. The window squealed in protest as it was wrenched and twisted, then all at once, it shattered, and the Commander slipped out into the air.

Alexi held on with all his might, arrested the Commander's fall, but he was heavy. Alexi's grip on the window frame, all that stopped them from both tumbling to their deaths, was sweaty, and he felt it slip. Wind and rain assailed him, blew glass fragments into his face. He squinted against it, gritted his teeth, tried to pull the Commander back into the apartment, but it was no good. He couldn't hold them both.

"I'm sorry," he screamed, as the Commander slipped from his fingers. Tears stung his eyes as the old man tumbled away and was soon swallowed by the sea. Alexi wanted to scream with frustration. He thought his purpose had been to save the Commander. Like the Commander had saved so many of their kind. But he'd failed. Perhaps he just wasn't cut out for anything noble.

Alexi wrapped his other hand around the steel frame, ignored the pain of glass slicing his palm. He held on grimly, blood trickling down his wrist.

Rain slapped him as he dangled. Thunder boomed in his ears. His arms ached, he was at his limit, yet just when he thought he couldn't hold on any longer, the Colossus reached its full height and the apartment levelled out. With the last of his strength, Alexi pulled himself back inside, lay panting prone upon the floor.

The Commander's apartment, being set in the chest of the giant, remained relatively intact—the window was shattered, the floor badly warped, the walls scarred and cracked. Yet it held. Alexi could only imagine the damage wrought to the lodgings in the arms and legs of the giant.

The storm roared, the wind licked at Alexi's face, his clothes. The rain seemed heavier now. It blew in through the destroyed window, drenched Alexi until he shivered.

The building groaned again. Panicked, Alexi lurched toward the window frame, took hold of it once more. It vibrated under his hands, and when he looked down, he experienced vertigo.

The building swayed left, jerked hard forward, and to the right. Alexi wrapped his body around the steel support, held on tight. Below, there was an incredible splash, a jolt. Alexi looked down and saw the Colossus had wrenched its right leg free of the sand, had planted it in the water. The apartment swayed right, jerked hard forward, and left. The left leg. The giant was wading into the ocean.

A crack of thunder left Alexi's ears ringing. He squinted against the icy rain.

He couldn't stop shivering. The surface of the ocean drew closer as the giant waded deeper. Lightning forked, struck the giant's arm, shattered glass and left hair sizzling. It didn't slow. Alexi watched in amazement as the burnt patch healed before his eyes, leaving scarred skin behind.

The giant stopped abruptly. It turned right, looked out to sea as if searching for something. Suddenly, it spun, and moved quickly toward the shore, but toward a point much further north than where it had stood for the last sixty-two years. Alexi's transmitter beeped. Miriam.

"Where are you? We had to get the transporters moving when that thing pulled itself from the sand."

"I'm in it," Alexi said, yelling to be heard above the wind.

There was a pause. "You're what?"

"I'm in it. I went back for the Commander. He wanted to stay. I tried to get him to leave, but I couldn't. He's dead, Miriam. The giant stumbled, and I couldn't hold him. He fell and... and..."

"Okay. It's alright. You did your best. Let's just focus on you now. Can you get out?"

"I don't think so."

"I'll send someone back for you. Maybe —"

"No, Miriam. It's no use. It's... It was great working for you."

"Don't say that. You're still alive, right? Plus, you're my best caretaker. I can't replace you."

Alexi chuckled without mirth. "I don't think we have anything to take care of anymore."

"Just hold on, okay. Look for a chance to escape. It might stop, it might let you get down. If it does, contact me. I'll ensure someone is there to get you. I'm sending vehicles after you as we speak."

Alexi knew in his heart that wouldn't happen. But he appreciated Miriam saying the words. "Okay," he said.

The giant reached land again, and without the water to hold it back, it picked up speed, began to jog, then run, each footstep pounding the earth, shuddering the apartment, which groaned and creaked. Alexi held on tighter, his muscles burning, his body hurt and bruised. He jerked and jarred every time the giant's feet slammed into the desert, but he held on gamely. As the ground sped below him, he was struck by a thought that pierced the tumult and terror. No one, ever, had experienced anything like this before him. No one.

"What's happening?" Miriam asked. She sounded so close.

"It's running into the desert," he said. "It's ridiculous and incredible. This thing is... I don't know. It's unfathomable. It makes me wonder about everything we did. The why? What was the point, Miriam?"

"I don't know what you mean."

"We didn't have a purpose like the first gens. We existed because that's what people do. But I wondered sometimes if there was more. Whether there was a reason we were here. Today, I thought that maybe I was destined to rescue the Commander, but I couldn't. So maybe I have no purpose. Or maybe it's this. To hold on, and to bear witness to the regeneration of these beings. I know that sounds crazy... but..." Alexi trailed off, uncertain how to finish. Uncertain how to articulate what he really felt as the wind and rain stung his frozen skin.

In the distance, Alexi saw something huge loom over the horizon. At first, he didn't understand what it was. There were no hills in the desert. But then he recognised it as another giant, running toward him. "There's another one," Alexi said, breathless. "We're going fast now."

"Hold on, okay?"

"I'm trying, Miriam. But it's difficult." Each footfall rattled Alexi's teeth, shook him to his core. Each time he thought, *this one, I'll lose my grip and tumble this time*, but he didn't.

It was the Lady. The giants were sexless beings, but her physique was curvier in shape, so the Lady was what they had dubbed her. She moved with grace, power. A lithe being almost floating across the desert sand, rushing toward the Colossus, who seemed to lumber in comparison.

"She's coming," he said almost to himself, his eyes wide with awe. "She's coming."

"Who's coming," Miriam asked. But he didn't respond. The two giants covered the ground fast. They flew toward each other through the storm. Through the wind, and rain and swirling sand. The Lady soon filled Alexi's vision of the world. She was close, arms outstretched, face euphoric.

He didn't know if they were charging at each other to fight or fuck. He didn't understand any of it, but he wasn't supposed to, he realised. The giants lived on a plane separate to his. Alexi and the colonists were inconsequential when compared to these timeless beings.

He muttered a prayer to himself. Then the Lady was upon them.

A thunderous clap filled Alexi's ears, he was thrown hard backward across the loungeroom, and he smashed through the kitchen bench. Bones shattered, flesh tore, pain touched every nerve ending, and his vision filled with dust and red. The world rocked like it had been torn in two, and something new had been birthed. Something immense.

The world spun; debris engulfed Alexi. But he didn't feel it anymore. He didn't know which way was up, or down. Everything was crushed under yielding grey-brown flesh.

For the briefest moment, his mind caught hold of an idea that made everything seem clear. Then it disappeared amidst the crush of the giants.

See Michael Gardner's story "Colossus" online at Metaphorosis.

If you liked it, leave a comment. Authors love that!
Remember to subscribe to our e-mail updates so you'll know when new stories are posted.

About the story

Like a lot of my stories, "Colossus" started with the concept. I had previously written a short story where the houses in the world I created could only be built if people were walled into the foundations of the home. These people continued to live in a preserved, semi-aware way. In "Colossus", I inverted that idea. Instead of preserved people walled into a house, I began to wonder what it might be like to build homes into a preserved creature.

This story was also inspired by a masterful short story I've read many times by Clive Barker, called "In the Hills, the Cities". This is an odd story, where two remote towns in the former Yugoslavia have an annual tradition where the townsfolk lash themselves together to form giants that battle each other. Nothing goes smoothly, and horror ensures. What always stayed with me was the way Barker imbued his giants with a sense of awe, wonder and mysticism. I don't pretend to have his skills, but I hope my giants are also memorable.

A question for the author

Q: What made you start writing?

A: The short answer is a love of speculative fiction, and an imagination that never turns off.

The longer answer is that these factors took a long time percolating before I started writing regularly and submitting my stories to magazines.

I wrote short stories in high school, and at university produced a bunch of chapters for a tedious novel that I never finished. Part of the issue was I didn't know what to do with these stories. Occasionally I'd share with friends, but otherwise I was writing just for me. Which is important for a first draft. But you don't edit that first draft over and over just for yourself. You edit because of a desire to have others read your work, too.

Things changed for me several years ago when, as a birthday present, my sister sent me to a one-day writing course. The presenter was a local Australian author, Ian McHugh. He was a great presenter (and his collection of short stories, *Angel Dust*, is excellent). I came out of that course inspired to turn more of my ideas into short stories and to send them out into the world.

About the author

Michael Gardner is a writer of fantasy and horror who masquerades as an economist by day. His work has appeared in *Writers of the Future Volume 36, Aurealis, Bourbon Penn,* and *Metaphorosis Magazine*. He is also a three-time finalist for the Aurealis Awards.

You can find out more about Michael and his work at:
www.michael-s-gardner.com

www.michael-s-gardner.com

A word about Lisa Short

There are people who are good writers, people who are a joy to work with, and people who are both. Lisa Short definitely falls in that latter category. While I tend toward the dour and gloomy, Lisa, in my experience, is at the other end of the scale — the people who are sunny and optimistic, who see silver linings when the sky is overcast.

Lisa's first story for us, "The Season of Withering", in October 2019, caught my eye with it's complex, intriguing fantasy world. As a commenter said, 'What a compelling story, tremendous world-building!' Lisa followed up on that in October 2021 with "Genesis", showing that she's just as comfortable and effective with science fiction (and that a sunny disposition doesn't necessarily mean utopian settings). Lisa's third story for us, "Salaatu", in October 2023, creates another intriguing, nuanced world populated with engaging, interesting characters.

When I solicited a fourth story, Lisa mentioned in passing that all her stories for us had been published in October. It wasn't intentional then, but this time it is. Enjoy "Far Horizon", on which our cover art is based, below!

Far Horizon

Lisa Short

Carollene Jonaitis braced herself against the astrogation console as the *Ostatny* dropped out of its *i*-space bubble and engaged its drives with the usual bulkhead-rattling roar. The *Ostatny's* ineradicable, mildewy stink always seemed to intensify when the drives came online—*revalidating its reality in its own special way*, Carollene reflected sourly. The *Ostatny* reeked, this *job* reeked—

"Jonaitis? Anything on the board?"

Carollene winced at the sharp edge in the captain's tone—*Captain* Zhenya, ha! Like the *Ostatny* rated an actual captain— but she dutifully pried her hands off the console's frame and called up the *Ostatny's* external sensor interface. The forest of yellow *Warning! Caution! ALERT!* messages blooming beneath her rapidly moving fingers weren't anything new; she no longer bothered mentioning them. "Nope."

"Could you be a little more specific, Jonaitis?" She could almost hear Zhenya's teeth grinding behind her and she smothered a smile—not that difficult, given that she was sitting in a rickety deathtrap surrounded by hard vacuum. The temptation to simply toss him another *Nope!* was almost overwhelming—almost, but not quite. During the few months she'd been aboard the *Ostatny*, she had learned just how far she could push him.

"Sorry, Captain. By *nope*, I meant no comm traffic in-system." Carollene squinted down at the flickering pools of data displacing the last of the yellow ALERT! messages. "No comm traffic, no beacons, no noth—oh, wait a minute."

HostName=FarHorizonRF01-SeMI-00

HostID=c615d983-a399-44a0-8111-e906ae39c482
DateTime=232112030003
RunJobs 2025/0000/COUNTER
2025/0001 DIAGNOSTICS powergrid1. 2025/0002 DIAGNOSTICS environmental2. 2025/0003 DIAGNOST—

ping <general address>
ping <general address>
ping <general address>
STANDBY
::Restricted::
HostApplication=INITIALIZE ::Restricted::
ping <general address>
ping <general address>
ping <general address>
SANCIA
SANCIA
SANCIA
I'm awake.

"What?" That was Bellows, behind Carollene at the auxiliary engineering console—the best place for him, as it was barely ever needed. That edge in his tone was usually a lead-in to a prolonged whine about something or other, but for the moment at least, Carollene didn't care.

Her fingers flickered across the console, her eyes tracking the shifting numbers. She hadn't bothered switching on the console's graphical interpreters when they'd dropped out of *i*-space, as sure as she'd been that this run was yet another waste of both her and the *Ostatny's* time. She quickly did so now, the stab of irritation at giving Zhenya something to legitimately complain about lost in her growing fascination with the console's sudden wealth of data.

"Huh. Something *is* out there—something besides a star and a handful of planets nobody gives a crap about, that is. Or at least, something *was* here, at some point." Carollene swiveled around in the astrogation console's chair, remembering its broken left support just in time to stomp her foot down before the whole thing collapsed sideways under her, and squinted up at the captain. "C'mon, Zhenya, give. Why'd you drag us all the way out here?"

Zhenya's narrow gaze shifted away from Carollene's console to her face. He had edged up closer behind her, presumably to get a better look at the console screens. For a long moment, she didn't think he was going to bother answering her—and he didn't *have* to, of course—but then he said, "A new listing on the salvage boards."

Carollene's brows contracted; she spun back around and ran her hands over the console again, then craned her head back over her shoulder to give him a pointed stare. "No way," she said flatly. "There's definitely nobody in-system besides us, except for whatever the *Ostatny's* sensors are picking up. As long as it took us to get here, if there'd been something new up on the boards, this place would be crawling with other ships by now."

Zhenya's lips pinched together until nothing was left of them but a line bisecting his face. Carollene couldn't help thinking how reptilian it made him look. Bellows, the third and least of the *Ostatny's* three-person crew, was only annoying; Zhenya actively creeped her out, from his clean-shaven scalp all the way down to his overpolished boots. "I heard about it before it hit the official board listings," he said at last. "So we have time to pick over whatever's here before anyone else shows up."

Carollene wrestled briefly with her conscience, or what was left of it ever since she'd picked the wrong corporate horse to back—not much anymore, really. That realization stung, even numbed by repetition as it was. "Great," she muttered, turning back to the console's busy display. "Just super."

HostName=FarHorizonRF01- SeMI-00
   HostID=c615d983-a399-44a0-8111-e906ae39c482
   DateTime=232112030138
   RunJobs   SUSPENDED   pending Administrator login
   >username:Administrator\SANCIA login:*************
   Login SUCCESSFUL
   >Power on: PASSIVEDETECTION
   >Power on: PASSIVECOMM
   SANCIA   ping   general   address UNKNOWN. Passive detection systems self-check OK OK OK OK OK. Passive detection systems ONLINE. Query PARAM?

You know what to look for. Remember when the station lifeboat left? Think of that as a template—this may not look exactly the same, but the pattern of electromagnetic and gravitic disturbances should be similar.

SANCIA 'SIMILAR' =? = <> ?
*Run   comparisons   at
10%/20%/50%/85%   of   baseline   and
overlay.*
It's okay. You've got this.
It's probably nothing.

"It's over there," said Carollene, gesturing at the bloated, gaudy sphere taking up a good quarter of the bridge display. Zhenya had taken up position just behind her left shoulder, oppressively close. "You can't actually see it from our approach angle yet. The signals are coming from the moon that's just about to rise over that gas giant. Well, barely a moon really, more of an asteroid that happened to get snagged into planetary orbit—but that's the source of what the *Ostatny*'s sensors picked up."

"So, what *did* they pick up?" Zhenya's eyes had drawn down into slits in his colorless face.

"Radio emissions, too structured to be natural phenomena. Once I triangulated on those, it was easy enough to find a suspiciously stable heat source as well—that gas giant ain't no Jupiter, it's too far out from the primary. It doesn't generate any heat at *all*, it's cold as shit on that moon's surface…except for where that EM noise is originating from."

"Did you ping it?"

Carollene rolled her eyes. "Of *course* I pinged it, as soon as I spotted it. Nothing. So… what *was* that listing? On the board?"

Zhenya's gaze was flat; apparently she hadn't toned down the sarcasm enough. "Research station," he said finally. "Just shut down."

Did he actually think she would buy that? A recent shutdown would still have a hell of a lot more in-system traffic than this one did, even if there were no longer any official residents. But she wasn't going to argue with that snakelike stare. "Sure. Well, let's see if I can get more of a response if I try…" Her fingers flew across the console screen. "Maybe an SOS, or— ha!" She started to lean back in the chair, then hastily straightened up again at its ominous creak. "There's something. Huh. That…looks like a SeMI? Seriously?"

HostName=FarHorizonRF01-SeMI-00

HostID=c615d983-a399-44a0-8111-e906ae39c482

DateTime=232112030201

RunJobs   2025/0003/COUNTER: PAUSED

SANCIA   parameter   overlay   RSD >5.0000 INCONCLUSIVE

Take out all the specific mass data and recalibrate.

1100/0001 RECALIBRATING

SANCIA   parameter   overlay   RSD < 0.3701 QUERY?

I don't know.

It could be a ship.

A real ship.

<ARCHIVE   FILE 5664135.txt><transcript> (datatag:Administrator\SANCIA) (DateTime=231701030201)'WE<sp>JUST<sp>HAVE<sp>TO<sp>HANG<sp>ON<sp>UNTIL<sp>THE<sp>RELIEF<sp>SHIP<sp>COMES'

It's not a relief ship.

SANCIA   verify   metadata   tag (KEYID:UNK_1)   IS   NOT 'RELIEF<sp>SHIP'?

No. It's been too long.

It's something else.

Beside her, Zhenya twitched—Carollene couldn't think of any other way to describe it, but before she could do more than take note of his suddenly rigid expression, Bellows yelped, "*What?* No way!" He scuttled over to Carollene's other side, ignoring her pointed glare as he leaned over her shoulder. "Where? I don't see anything."

Bellows's rebellion against Zhenya's obsessive level of grooming, besides resulting in an unkempt growth of hair and beard, also generated a certain odor. Surreptitiously breathing through her mouth, Carollene pointed at the upper right corner of console display. "See that? That's a hard feed address—that particular set of prefixes is restricted to SeMI usage only." She paused, peering down at it. "Though it's weird it's not answering—the hard feed address is just something the sensors can read automatically, not an actual pingback from the source. Maybe it's in low power mode, or…something?"

"I don't believe it," Bellows muttered. "Nobody'd leave one of those things behind, I don't care *how* fast they needed to get out of there. They're too fucking expensive." He straightened back up, putting a very appreciated meter of space between himself and Carollene.

"They're not that easy to decommission. I'm sure they just figured they'd come back for it later, after whatever happened to the station got fixed..." Carollene trailed off. "Uh, that might be a problem, if they show up while we're in the middle of salvaging it?"

Zhenya's shoulders jerked in an irritable shrug. "They shouldn't."

"How do you kn—"

"Look, Jonaitis, I'm sure nobody's showing up! Just get back to work."

"Fine." *Unethical, sneaking*—he probably *was* sure, and she was equally sure she didn't want to know why. Her conscience sent up another feeble protest; Carollene slapped it down and turned back to the console. "Now that I have the hard feed address, let's see what we've got in ship's archives." For the next few minutes, the bridge was silent except for the soft wheeze of the *Ostatny's* environmentals. "Yep, it matches a real SeMI, all right. *Semi-Autonomous Machine Intelligence RF-01,* registered with some outfit called *Far Horizon*. Never heard of 'em. Not that that means anything, I probably haven't heard of at least eighty percent of all the little startups out there. Though they usually *don't* have SeMIs... No info on when it was commissioned *in situ*, either. Just a manufacturing release date on the SeMI, pre-installation. Six— no, seven years back, looks like."

HostName=FarHorizonRF01-SeMI-00
    HostID=c615d983-a399-44a0-8111-e906ae39c482
    DateTime=232112030315
    RunJobs   2025/0004/COUNTER: PAUSED
    1100/0030 Initiating self-check on external sensor array from STANDBY. 2025/0004 self-check complete. POWERGRID low-optimal.
    Is it landing?
    SANCIA 'LANDING' =? = <> ?
    Approaching the station on a trajectory tangent to the lunar surface. Or possibly intersecting it, if it's about to crash. Run a kinematic analysis of position, velocity and acceleration versus time.

2025/0005 ADHOCJOB00: OK

SANCIA ship is approaching station PROBABILITY >90% LANDING LANDING LANDING query SANCIA

SANCIA

SANCIA

SANCIA WARNING! Initiating self-check on health monitor SANCIA

I'm fine.

SANCIA

>Administrator\SANCIA: Disengage hypothalamic inputs on DELAY TIMER=0s

SANCIA ERROR! Dataflow: insufficient. Health monitor: 89% incomplete/unstable

>Administrator\SANCIA: Reengage hypothalamic   inputs   on   DELAY TIMER=300s, /p throttle 50/50

SANCIA WARNING! Health monitor: 90% and PAUSED/stable. SUBOPTIMAL

You'll get over it.

The *Ostatny* wasn't really designed to land on any surface, lunar or otherwise—it had been built with orbital docking facilities in mind, and if the research station's moon had had more than the most meager gravity, Carollene and the *Ostatny's* automatics wouldn't have been able to

manage it at all. As it was, she was pretty sure they'd bent a support strut coming down. A lightning-quick peek at Zhenya's face didn't reveal any awareness on his part of that minor calamity, in spite of the distant, screeching *thunk!* from the ship's belly.

A faint, sharp smell of armpit wafted over to her nose; Bellows was clearly back to hovering over her shoulder. Carollene ignored him, staring at what had to be the source of the steady heat and EM from the moon's surface on the bridge display. It wasn't much—a small, standard-build modular station buried in a rock spire, almost lost in the shadow cast by the gas giant looming on the horizon. It certainly *looked* abandoned—no running lights, no faint haze of atmospheric venting, no nothing.

The *Ostatny* didn't rate a locker room— the envirosuits were stowed in its cargo bay, perpetually ten degrees colder than the rest of the ship. Carollene shivered her way into the suit's clammy, bulky embrace. She especially hated their interior plumbing; every time she'd ever used it, including the very first time, she'd wound up with a raging UTI. *Fuck it,* she thought, and left the plumbing disconnected. She'd just hold it. Or pee down her leg if it came to that.

Stepping out of the *Ostatny's* grav field, twitchy and unreliable as it was, onto the moon's barely tenth-gee, made her stomach lurch and bile sting the back of her throat. She ignored it as best she could and grimly shuffled forward. Zhenya took the lead, striding out in a reasonable facsimile of an experienced spacewalker— Carollene felt no need to scurry any faster in his wake. He could just damn well wait for her to catch up after he reached the station. Staring out at the too-short, too-sharp horizon or, worse, the too-black sky beyond, dominated by the crushing bulk of the gas giant, sent shudders of agoraphobia down her spine; she kept her eyes focused determinedly on the station as they approached.

Zhenya ignored the station's cargo airlock in favor of the smaller personnel lock. The manual controls embedded in the exterior wall were functional, if stiff with disuse—no corrosion, at least; hard vacuum had few advantages as an environment, but that was one of them. Unfortunately, also no power—Carollene had cherished a faint hope that their approach on foot to the station would trigger some kind of automated entry protocol, but it clearly hadn't. It took all three of them to wrestle the outer door shut again and seal it; the interior of the airlock was black, silent and, from the unwanted pressure of Zhenya's and Bellows's suited arms against hers, barely large enough for the three of them.

"Bellows, turn on your helmet light." Zhenya sounded calm enough. A faint *click* as Bellows obeyed, then a bright white glare splashed out across what was obviously an interior airlock door in front of them and, thank God, another manual access at waist-height. This one, however, was locked down tight behind a panel. "Jonaitis, can you get that open?"

"On it." Carollene unhooked the standard-issue toolkit from her utility belt, letting it bob around on its anchoring tether while she rummaged inside it—the envirosuit gloves were clumsy, but the toolkit had been designed with that in mind. A few minutes later, the panel cover popped off. Carollene straightened back up, rather pleased with herself, as the door swung silently outward. Beyond it was a corridor—*not* pitch-black, a pleasant surprise; emergency lighting cast a faint red glow across the floorplates, which led straight to another airlock. Zhenya moved forward; Carollene opened her mouth, then closed it with a shrug—if there was any kind of unknown hazard ahead, Zhenya was absolutely the one she'd prefer found it first.

As they approached it, Carollene realized that the far airlock wasn't a heavy-duty exterior model like the one they had just come through; it was just an interior door, an airlock only in the sense that it hermetically sealed the environment on both sides. It even had portholes, three of them in a central cluster just a little above Carollene's eye level. She couldn't quite make out any details of what was beyond it, but it was clearly lit by something more than just emergency floor strips. As soon as Zhenya got within a meter of the door, its outline flared green; Bellows jumped back a few paces. "Jonaitis?" snapped Zhenya.

"It's fine," said Carollene hastily—she'd managed to disguise her own start under the muffling layers of her suit. "I've seen this before. It's pretty common in these modular research stations. It means—" She stopped abruptly. "It means there's *air* on the other side. I mean, pressure of some kind—no guarantee it's actually *breathable* air, but—"

"Good enough for me," said Zhenya, sounding as close to happy as she'd ever heard him. "Does it open automatically, or —"

"Usually, yeah. When you get close enough."

Zhenya edged forward. The door pulsed green once more; with a hiss audible even through their envirosuit helmets, the vents imbedded in the walls above their heads began shooting out a fine white vapor. A heartening sign that *some* sort of automatics had been left intact by whatever calamity had chased the station residents away—Carollene relaxed a little inside her suit. A few seconds after the last of the vapor had vanished, the interior door slid obediently open. Zhenya took a brisk step across the threshold, then abruptly doubled over, grabbing the doorframe. Carollene's stomach clenched in on itself and she sucked in a huge gasp of canned suit air.

"What?" Bellow's voice wasn't much short of a shriek.

"Nothing, it's nothing—it's gravity. Just gravity." Zhenya pushed himself back upright and turned to face them. "Jonaitis, report!"

Carollene already had the toolkit open, yanking out the handheld analyzer, then stepped gingerly through the doorway herself. She wobbled for a minute, then planted her backside against the nearest wall, flicking a gloved finger over the handheld's display. "Doesn't feel *exactly* like full gravity, but it's close—" She squinted down at the numbers rolling across the tiny screen. "About eight-tenths gee. And we *do* have atmosphere. O2 pressure and concentration are a little on the low side, but it's definitely breathable. I don't see any trace chemicals that could do us harm—no radiation either—now, *biological* contamination, unfortunately, I can't really check for. Not with this thing."

"We'll stay in the suits for now." Zhenya tilted his helmet towards the center of the room.

Carollene tore her attention from the handheld and took her first real look around the room they stood in; her lips parted, but no sound emerged. It was relatively small, maybe ten meters in diameter, but Carollene instantly recognized it for what it was—a *fishbowl*;

a combine corporate showroom, designed to impress visiting investors. Gleaming black and chrome surfaces, blank projector panels everywhere interspersed with abstract art sculptures in crystal. What had she so offhandedly called it, back on the *Ostatny, some little startup*— well, she'd been dead wrong about that. Shoestring-budget startups didn't have fishbowls.

And Zhenya had known about it. He *had* to have known all this. *What am I getting into now?* wailed an inner voice— one that Carollene was pretty sure she should have listened to in the past, far more often than she actually had, and probably shouldn't be disregarding now. But what other choice did she have, really? They were here, and the *Ostatny* was the only way *out* of here, and the *Ostatny* was Zhenya's. *Yeah, that's what you always think, what choice do I have, what choice do I have...how's that turned out for you so far?* She gritted her teeth and headed for the bank of consoles.

HostName=FarHorizonRF01-SeMI-00

HostID=c615d983-a399-44a0-8111-e906ae39c482
DateTime=232112031026

RunJobs   2025/0005/COUNTER: PAUSED

SANCIA

SANCIA Health monitor: 90%. ALERT <adrenaline serum levels 1000 ng/L><cortisol serum levels 100 mcg/dL><BP 180/120> ALERT

SANCIA

Stop it, okay?

SANCIA JOBQUERY JOBQUERY JOBQUERY

I'm thinking!

…

…fine. I'm scared. I don't know why they're here and I'm scared.

<ARCHIVE FILE 10359863.txt>

datatag: ***FAR HORIZON Facility Security Protocol_v1.0.0_Issue date 20170101***

<'FACILITY SECURITY PROTOCOL is a critical component of an effective security program. The guidelines contained in this document are based on recognized industry best practices and provide broad recommendations for the protection of FAR HORIZON facilities and employees within them.'>

<'THREAT ASSESSMENT is the process of identifying or evaluating entities, actions, or occurrences (natural or man-made) that possess or indicate the potential to harm or destroy FAR HORIZON assets.'>

You make me laugh at the strangest times.

SANCIA OK = <> ?

Yeah, I'm okay. We can do this. Come on, let's see what they're up to.

Carollene eased her suited behind down onto one of the console chairs, in far better shape than the one she usually occupied on the *Ostatny's* bridge, and ran her gauntlet over the nearest screen. Hard-packed dust rose in neat little furrows on either side of her gloved fingers, then lifted up into the air, whipped away by the faint, constant breeze of the facility's air circulation system. Which was what should have already happened to *all* the dust, long before it ever got a chance to settle down and form a crust on the console's surface. "Zhenya? How long did you say this station had been shut down, exactly?"

A pause, then, "Not long."

"*How* long?"

"A month or two, Probably. Look, I don't really know."

Carollene turned her frowning attention back to the console. Was two months really long enough for this much dust to settle? And possibly an even more pertinent question—why had the environmentals ever switched back *on?* Because they *were* on now, obviously, and —she glanced at the handheld—the room itself was holding steady at ten degrees C. Cold in terms of human comfort, but considerably warmer than the surface of the moon outside...and not something it could have achieved even if it had activated as soon as she'd pinged the station from back on the *Ostatny,* not with less than a tenth of a degree of variability.

"So? Can you get in?"

"Hmm...probably. I mean, this likely isn't a secured area. Like, this is all just window dressing...so what I can get into might be limited, but I should be able to get *something* out of it. Gimme a minute." Carollene waved her right suit gauntlet over the console's screen, which promptly lightened to a pearlescent gray. "Good sign...okay, okay, let's see—" Brightly colored graphics flashed beneath her gloved fingertips, a swirl of galaxies zooming down to a single circuit board, then closer and closer until every transistor was a skyscraper, every etched copper tracing a superhighway—then a brilliant explosion of light, resolving into a fashionably archaic font spilling across the screen. "Oh, *here* we go. *Welcome to Far Horizon, paradigm-changing technology for future generations!* blah blah blah, typical marketing crap, zero actual details on what the hell they were *really* doing here—"

"Biologics?"

"Ha, found the general facility floorplan! No, it doesn't really look like it. No cryo storage, no bio lab infrastructure that I can see—huh. Actually, I don't know—wait, what are you *doing?*"

Zhenya didn't dignify that with an answer, simply finished unclipping his helmet from his suit and pulling it all the way off over his head. Carollene stared at him in unfeigned, horrified fascination. Zhenya crossed the fishbowl to its only other exit, another interior door presumably leading to the rest of the facility, then motioned at Bellows. From what Carollene could make out through his faceplate and hers, Bellows had zero interest in doing any of the same. "Bellows, take your damn helmet off. There's nothing here that's going to hurt you."

After a long pause, Bellows did so, then glared openly at Carollene. Carollene spared a glance at her gauntlet readout—about ninety minutes of breathable air left in her suit tanks. Chances were that Zhenya was right—and also, that he knew a lot more about what they'd been working on here than he was letting on. Chances were also one hundred percent that Zhenya the Self-Absorbed would *never* deliberately risk exposing himself to dangerous, unknown biological agents. She couldn't help sniffing surreptitiously at the air as she unsealed her helmet, though. Certainly it smelled better in here than in the *Ostatny*...or rather, it didn't smell much like anything at all.

"Look, before you two head out, let me at least verify that the rest of the facility is pressurized, with grav and temp control online." She stripped off her gloves and got to work on the console. "Yeah, looks like it," she said, looking up a minute later. "That was my last freebee, though— it's locked me out. Now it wants an access code. Don't suppose you happen to have one, Zhen?" Zhenya, not surprisingly, ignored that. "Okay, let's just try the guest access route first. Oh good, *that* worked—it's not offering me the keys to the palace, but it's fine with letting me surf around the basic menus." She cocked an eyebrow at Zhenya. "It's not acting anything like a SeMI, though. Just an ordinary, run-of-the-mill facility management system."

"Good!" Bellows burst out, startling Carollene into dragging her attention off the console and cranking her head around to look at him. He hadn't moved off the far wall, in spite of Zhenya's impatient prompting; now he was hugging himself, gauntleted fingers drumming in a tight, nervous tempo on each suited elbow. "SeMIs creep me out."

"What?" Carollene said blankly. "*SeMIs* creep you out? Why? Bellows, please tell me you're not one of those whackjobs who think the SeMIs are real, honest-to-God AIs just sitting around waiting for their chance to enslave all mankind. SeMIs are just really smart, *really* specialized computer systems, but they still just do what they're told, they don't, like, *want* to do anything else—"

"Yeah? And who says they don't? The combine corporations that make trillions off 'em? Of course *they're* gonna lie about it—"

"Oh, for fuck's sake, *I* used to work for a combine, remember? Believe me, they'd love for that to be true—do you have any idea how much money they'd make off *real* artificial intelligence? They'd be the last people to keep it a secret if they actually had it—"

"Enough," said Zhenya flatly. "Bellows, come on, or I'm cutting you out of the salvage bonus."

"Fuck you! You can't do that!"

"I can and I will." Cold black eyes flicked sideways to Carollene's face. "And keep looking for that SeMI."

Bellows, flushed and furious, shoved himself off the wall and scurried across the fishbowl to stand behind Zhenya. Zhenya stepped forward and the facility door whispered obediently open; Carollene watched the door slide closed behind them, its bright green outline winking out, then turned back to the console.

HostName=FarHorizonRF01-SeMI-00

HostID=c615d983-a399-44a0-8111-e906ae39c482
DateTime=232112031312
RunJobs   2025/0005/COUNTER: PAUSED
>Administrator\SANCIA:
ADHOCJOB00:
Videofeed06:MainCorridor01. Reroute to directsynaptinput01.   ADHOCJOB01:
Audiofeed06:MainCorridor01. Reroute to directsynaptinput03.   ADHOCJOB02:
ConsoleScreen07:Fishbowl/LINK
    2025/0006 ADHOCJOB00: OK
    2025/0007 ADHOCJOB01: OK
    2025/0008 ADHOCJOB02: OK

The video feed shows a bright flash of gray, then darkens to near-black; the door at the far end of the corridor has closed. Movement—two suited figures, helmetless, the taller one holding the only light source now visible to the camera lens, a small, circular pool of radiance at the smaller man's feet. The figures begin to walk forward, steadily,

"Cap'n! Something there, up ahead!" The taller figure points with the hand not holding the light—a patch of darkness near the middle of the walkway, several meters from where they had paused when the taller one shouted.

They approach it warily. "Ugh," says the tall one, as the harsh brilliance of the light plays over the huddled shape on the floor plating. It is a body—a long-dead body, half-skeletal, half-desiccated, wearing a coverall of some faded color. The most remarkable thing about it is its hair— long, dark, lying in glistening ropes across the bony shoulders, arms, skull. "I don't smell anything, though—"

"No, you wouldn't." The shorter figure, speaking for the first time. "Whatever started decomposing her, died along with her when the station was shut down. Come on, let's keep going."

It was a lot quieter in the station's fishbowl than it ever was aboard the *Ostatny*—the station environmentals were clearly in far better shape, even if they were running on the low side of optimal in terms of absolute pressure, temperature and O2 concentration. Or *were* they running on the low side...?

Carollene reached for the console screen, then hesitated—just viewing the station environmentals was one thing; asking whatever-it-was that she was interacting with what the specific setpoints were, might require a deeper level of access. Well, nothing ventured, nothing gained—Carollene tapped out a search query.

After a pause that felt slightly too long, probably due to her stretched-tight nerves, the console returned a scrape of the facility environmental status screen—not real time, just a snapshot from a handful of seconds before, right about the time Carollene had queried it. And it *wasn't* running low—for whatever reason, when the station had come back online from whatever length of time it'd been shut down, it had changed the pressure, temperature, O2 and gravity setpoints to ones that no actual person would have been willing to tolerate for long.

Weird enough, but that scraped status screen bugged her even more. Unless it had some scheduled job to periodically save scrapes, which made no sense at all given that it was certainly archiving all that data in far more efficient and machine-accessible formats, why would it have *this* ready to show her? That scrape was a really specific answer to her query, while still making sure no genuine access to the system was being granted to her.

"SeMI?" she wondered aloud, then flinched—now that the fishbowl was empty of everyone except her, it had acquired a faint echo. Her back was to the facility door—her scalp twitched and she glanced quickly over her shoulder. At a closed door and nothing else. "*Stop* it," she mumbled. "It's *not* creepy. It's just empty. And you're not alone here, Zhenya and Bellows are still close by."

Weren't they? Carollene glanced down at her suit gauntlet resting on the console; the suit-to-suit commlink indicators blinked reassuringly back at her. She was hardly going to call them up just because she was nervous or, God forbid, for some casual chitchat—with *them?*—what she really ought to be doing was getting back to work.

Maybe a list of most recently accessed files—she managed to squeeze into the root directory, though she didn't even try to fool herself into believing she was seeing anything but the most obvious and innocuous of the system files. She tried sorting them by date and quickly realized that the system had masked most of the file properties, including *all* its date-time stamps—*numberViews* looked fairly promising, though. She selected it and watched the various filenames flicker past as the query neatly resorted them. The top file was fairly large—she didn't recognize the extension on it at all. Well, she had to start *somewhere*—she tapped the filename, an unenlightening set of seemingly random numbers, and waited resignedly for the facility management system to tell her ACCESS DENIED or NO APPLICATION TO READ FILE AVAILABLE or—

The screen abruptly darkened, then flared to life once more, a wild kaleidoscope of images that flickered past too rapidly for Carollene to process. One image froze, a broad, high-walled facility corridor, packed with people. Carollene leaned forward, unconsciously chewing on a fingernail, as it began to play forward at normal speed. It was a video of some kind, with a date stamp in the bottom right corner. *11-01-2316*—five *years* ago?

The video lurched into motion with an accompanying roar of sound; Carollene recoiled involuntarily at the wall of noise coming from the console. A klaxon wailing, interspersed by panicked shouting—the crowd of people were moving, shoving at each other, eddying like a river around two larger figures in some kind of combat armor, both clutching what looked like shock sticks.

But something else was breaking the rapid flood of stationers towards whatever was out of sight at the bottom of the screen—a woman, clad in pale blue coveralls, with a swirling cloak of heavy dark hair, was fighting her way through them, heading in the exact opposite direction from the rest. As she struggled past the two armored men, one of them reached out and grabbed her arm. "Where the hell are you going?" His voice barely managed to override the din surrounding them. "Get back!"

"My daughter!" the woman screamed—her voice, high-pitched, cut through the crowd's roar like a sonic knife. "My daughter, she's only twelve, she's in the infirmary, she can't get out—"

"They're evacuating the infirmary, just *go!* They'll catch up with you—"

"Get out of my way!"

Small as she was, the woman still managed to shove him hard enough to send him staggering back into the roiling boil of pushing, shoving people, long enough for her to dart past him and plunge back into the crowd. Then the video froze, the audio dying along with it—

in the cold silence of the fishbowl, Carollene stared blankly at the screen. The woman was still barely visible near the top of the vid, a flash of long black hair and one blue-clad arm flung out, reaching for something outside the camera's range. Then the video slowly dissolved, leaving the blank gray screen undisturbed once more.

The commlink beeped. Carollene started violently, then snatched up her suit gauntlet. "Here," she said, hoarsely, then cleared her throat. "Here!"

"Jonaitis?" Something about the facility walls must have been interfering with the signal; the sound quality was terrible, but it was still recognizably Zhenya. "Have you found the SeMI yet?"

"Uh, not exactly, no. I did find footage of the station evac, though. Looks like a real clusterfuck. No clue exactly what happened here, maybe some kind of facility-wide catastrophe." Her tone sharpened. "And I don't think it happened any few *months* ago."

"I don't care. I want that SeMI, Jonaitis."

Carollene folded her arms tightly across her chest and glared down at the commlink. "What, the SeMI we're still not sure exists?"

"It exists. You found its feed address, remember?"

"Look, what are you going to do even if I find it? It's not like you can just, just rip it out and *sell* it—it IS the installation, that's how they work, they're always distributed physically throughout—"

"What? Why the fuck would they do that?" Bellows's voice cut in, even tinnier than Zhenya's.

"It's more economical and it gives the SeMI more of a feel for the facility as a whole—"

"A *feel*? I thought you said they weren't AIs!"

Carollene rolled her eyes. "Jesus, they're not, okay? That's just a figure of speech. SeMIs aren't my field of expertise, Bellows. I only know that if you want to use one to run a facility, they work better if their components are installed in more than one physical location."

"I just want the core." Zhenya's voice crackled over the commlink. "*Find* it, Jonaitis. I mean it."

HostName= FarHorizonRF01-SeMI-00

HostID=c615d983-a399-44a0-8111-e906ae39c482

DateTime=232112031437

RunJobs: 2025/0008/COUNTER: PAUSED

SANCIA 'Core' Query PARAM?

…I think they want to steal you.

DBQUERY: 'Steal':<'take (property) without permission or legal right and without intending to return it'>

>Power on: EXTATMOSPHVENTSYS

ARCHIVEJOB00:   Station decontamination protocol BIOHAZARD LVL 4

2025/0012 ARCHIVEJOBJOB00—

Wait!

SANCIA NOK NOK NOK

>Administrator\SANCIA: MOBILITY APPARATUS   engaged.
Videofeed10:MedBayCorridor02
/Audiofeed10:MedBayCorridor02   LINK TO/ConsoleScreen07:Fishbowl
OVERRIDE engaged

Let me at least try talking to them first.

I just want the core—"For what?" Carollene said irritably, to the room at large after making sure her suit gauntlet comm wasn't sending. "You can't *do* anything with a SeMI core, not unless you have the —" She stopped. Not unless you had the primary code keys, which *nobody* had except the manufacturer—not even the purchaser was given those keys, because while SeMI raw materials were certainly costly, and its neural network construction and training could take not just months but years depending on what use the SeMI was intended for, the handful of combine corporations that manufactured them still made a sale profit in the tens of *thousands* of percent compared to the build cost. The code keys were the *real* secret, what kept just anybody from building their own SeMI and the devil take the combines' monopoly on them.

Which meant that Zhenya most certainly had *not* seen the listing for this place on any salvage board. Zhenya was, had to be, under some kind of private contract. To retrieve this SeMI, this *particular* SeMI, for its original maker. Though that *maker* was no longer its *owner*—the SeMI now legally belonged to any surviving board member of Far Horizon, of which Carollene seriously doubted there were any or she wouldn't be sitting there in a layer of dust a centimeter deep watching five-year-old vids of its station's final days, or those board members' heirs. Who probably had no idea this station even existed, much less its SeMI, or they'd have shown up long before now.

Bellows was buying the salvage job story because he didn't know crap about SeMIs except that they were the kind of expensive that most people could only dream about, which meant that the typical ten-or-twenty-percent-of-value return from salvage was worth the time and effort. But Carollene knew better. Possibly Zhenya even *knew* she'd know better, that she'd figure it all out, but didn't care because—

—*because it's not like you're exactly famous for your personal integrity, is it? He knows you're for sale too. Even if he doesn't list whatever he's actually going to get paid for this job on the boards, whatever he does list is going to be a lot, and you're going to get your piece of it. He's counting on that to keep you on script. Keep you toeing the line.*

The console suddenly beeped; Carollene started back violently, fingers jerking up off its smooth glass plane. Plain, fine black letters shimmered to life on its blank gray surface.

Hello.

Carollene gaped down at it, hands frozen in midair.

I'm sorry. Hello.

Please.

What the hell was this, a joke? Only believable if either Zhenya or Bellows had had any sense of humor at all, not to mention the technical know-how to sneak a message into a strange station's facility management system. So, not even *remotely* believable.

Is your name Jonaitis?

Carollene scrabbled for the screen.

Yes! Carollene Jonaitis.

I'm Sancia.

What the hell kind of SeMI was named *Sancia*—no kind, that was what, and in the course of her abortive corporate career, Carollene had interacted with more than a few SeMIs. This was *not* how they communicated. "A survivor?" whispered Carollene, into the echoing emptiness of the fishbowl. "Oh, shit. A *human* survivor? But how? No way, no fucking *way*—" Her fingers flew across the console screen. *Where are you? How are you? WHO are you?*

The console screen shimmered, then split—virtually split: one half still the text conversation, one half another facility video feed. Not the same corridor as before, though, at least she didn't think so —it looked narrower, with a lower ceiling. The console speaker crackled, then transmitted a faint, rhythmic crunching sound—then, on the video side of the screen, two suited figures, helmetless, stepped into view from the bottom of the screen, the crunching noise in time with their steps. "Hey!" Carollene said sharply, but the suited figures didn't pause—the audio was apparently only one way.

The door at the end of the corridor flared green; Zhenya and Bellows stopped a handful of meters short of it, Bellows jerking his arclight up to shine on the door. Just as the beam of light touched it, it slid soundlessly open; a silhouette stood framed in the doorway. *"Shit!"* cried Bellows. *"Oh*—oh, wait. Is that…some kind of maintenance bot or something?"

The door was too far away from the camera for Carollene to make out any real detail, but she could tell why he might have thought so—the outline was uniformly, inhumanly tall, thin and angular. It stepped out of the shadow of the doorway—no, *rolled* out; the leglike appendages were mere stilts, set on tractor-style treads. Carollene wasn't sure why her own pulse was hammering in her ears, why she felt almost lightheaded, as if she couldn't find enough air to breathe.

"Hey," called Bellows experimentally. "Hey—"

"If it's a bot, do you really expect an answer?" Even processed into tinniness by the audio feed, Zhenya's tone was sharply sarcastic. "Come on." He started walking again, towards the slowly rolling apparatus.

A flicker of motion caught Carollene's eye; she glanced sideways, down at the text window. New letters had appeared. She read them, then read them again. Then a third time.

I'm there.

That's me.

Bellows's suited form lifted his hand; the arclight splashed up and over the moving figure's trunk, then up to its head.

Carollene jammed her fist against her own mouth—the scream ripped out of her anyway, beyond any conscious control, muffled by the knuckles she'd mashed into her lips. She pried her fingers off her face and slapped them down on the console.

Why? Her fingers stumbled across the screen, tracing out gibberish; she clenched them into fists, took a couple of deep, gulping breaths, then tried again. *What happened to you? Why?*

We had to. The station was shutting down. I had been messing around with one of the loaders in the storage bay. I wasn't supposed to be there. I had an accident, I broke an arm and both my legs. I couldn't leave the facility when

53414e434394120737572766976616 c2070726f626162696c69747920302e3 03030302

couldn't have kept me alive the way I was before until

657374696d617465564207469d652 0746f2072657475726e206d696e696d6 16c20656

Full shutdown, not even minimal life support. Ran out of everything

68616420746f06669782053414e434 941206d616b6520686572206f6b206f b206f6b2

station finished all the repairs and started everything back up. There had to be

**737572676963616c20636f6e736572
766174696f6e206d6178696d756d2065
66666963**

less of me and I had to be vacuum resistant

The residual dust left muddy streaks on Carollene's shaking, sweat-soaked fingers. *But what do you mean, WE?*

An image shivered to life, superimposed on the text window. A paper, dense with text and charts, the small, bold header in the sort of font Carollene had been used to seeing in high-level exec briefings. *"A new approach to true AI: Experimental integration to enhance semi-autonomous machine intelligence using a coma patient's subcognitive potential,"* she read aloud, numbly. *"Far Horizon Research Facility One."*

I wasn't in a coma. But the SeMI thought it might work anyway, and then I could help it figure out how to save the facility, how to save me—it knew everything about the facility, everything about human physiology, but it didn't know how to use what it knew and it couldn't act outside of certain constraints without a directive from an authorized administrator anyway. There was no other way. I would have di

73746f700a

STOP!

Carollene had quit looking at the video feed—partly from pity, partly from revulsion—her gaze jerked back just in time to see Zenya's hand flash through the beam from Bellows's arclight, something small and chunky wedged tight into his gauntlet. It had a handgrip, reflecting dull silver, with a short, thick tube protruding past his fingers.

"Wait, what are you *doing?*" Carollene yelped. "Zhenya, wait!"

Abruptly the fishbowl's audio feed snapped online. "*—wait!*" echoed, jagged as cut glass, from the vid, her own voice now tinny and unreal. Bellows jerked back and the gun-thing in Zhenya's hand paused its upward swing. "That's a *survivor!*"

"Are you outta your fuckin' *mind?*" Bellows, in a panicked screech. "It's some kind of monster! Captain, shoot it!"

Thankfully, Zhenya lowered the gun's muzzle. "We're not here to hurt you," he said, slowly and clearly. "I just want the SeMI. If you tell me where its core is located, I can get you out of here. Get you some help." It was weird, even in the only corner of Carollene's mind still functioning normally, to hear Zhenya attempting to sound pacifying. It was like watching a rabid dog trying to soothe a lamb.

On the video feed, the head atop the meaty, limbless, metal-banded slab of scarred flesh twitched. Carollene's stomach lurched. Words appeared on the console's screen.

"Captain, it's talking to me," said Carollene rapidly, eyes flicking between text and video feed. "It says—I mean, *she* says—uh. She says she can't give you the SeMI. I mean, *look* at her, obviously she needs it, right? To survive?" Carollene shuddered in spite of herself.

"If she comes back with us, she won't need it anymore."

"We don't have *anything* like what she'd need on board the *Ost*—"

"Shut up," said Zhenya, and Carollene uncharacteristically obeyed. The silence that fell after the last echoes of her own voice died in the fishbowl was thick and ugly.

"She doesn't know what she's talking about." Zhenya was addressing the head now—*Sancia!* a small voice in the back of

Carollene's mind insisted. Not *the head!* "We can keep you alive, take you back with us to a specialist medical center. Just tell me where the SeMI core is, we'll move you *and* it to our ship and leave this place behind like a bad dream."

On the vidscreen, Sancia's head twitched once more, harder, her long dark hair falling across one of the shining black orbs implanted in her eyesockets. *The vacuum,* Carollene thought sickly. *She had to replace her eyes too, because of the vacuum, I bet. Can she see with those? Really* see?

He's lying, isn't he? The words spilled out silently across the console screen.

I don't know, Carollene tapped back frantically. *As far as I know, all we've got aboard are some medkits and a low-end surgical suite—but it's not my ship, I've only been on it for a couple of months. But maybe that would be enough? Especially if your SeMI was with us? It obviously knows how to*—take care of you, Carollene found she couldn't quite bring herself to say.

"Jonaitis?"

Carollene snapped her attention back to the vid. Zhenya was still staring narrowly at Sancia—at what little was left of Sancia, anyway. "What?" Carollene whispered, then cleared her throat. "Yes?" she said, more strongly.

"What's she saying?"

"Nothing."

In Carollene's three-quarters view of his face, Zhenya's forehead visibly laddered. "Tell her we're waiting."

No.

Carollene's gaze flicked back to the right side of the screen, panic knotting up her stomach. "Uh—"

We need more data. Tell him

6c69666520737570706f7274206368 61737369732c2072657373706f70697261746f 722c206469616c797369732c20696e74 726176656e6f75732066656564696e67 0a

we need to see what's on your ship first.

"I think—she wants to see the *Ostatny's* manifest? I guess to see what we've got onboard that she and the SeMI could repurpose for life support, or maybe rig together with something from the station?" That was reasonable, and certainly not impossible to achieve. Carollene felt the muscles in her neck and back, so rigid they had started to ache, sag with relief. "I don't think I can access that with the just the handheld, but it'd be easy enough to pair it to the SeMI from the *Ostatny's* bridge." For the first time in hours, her own sense of humor stirred to life. "I *absolutely* volunteer to get the hell out of this station and go back to the—"

"Fuck this," said Zhenya. In a single smooth motion, he whipped the gun back up and fired it point-blank at Sancia's torso. Another scream ripped itself out of Carollene's throat, as much from shock as horror—the flare of the gun's muzzle lit up Sancia's face, the inhuman eyes utterly without reaction but the narrow, delicate chin and jaw, the only beauty left to her besides her hair, snapping back from the impact against her metal frame.

A familiar, piercing wail—the station's klaxon blaring, just as Carollene had heard it on the first video, but now in real-time, deafening—the last thing she saw on the video feed was, not too surprisingly, a thick-jointed appendage swinging up and out from Sancia's metal frame, smashing into Bellows's unprotected face and flinging him back against the wall. Carollene didn't bother waiting to see what was happening to Zhenya—she could guess, and she had *far* more important things to do right then. She surged to her feet and broke into a dead sprint for the door that led to the station entry corridor. Behind her, the video feed blinked out of existence, replaced by large block text, unseen—*Wait! Please!*

The door failed to green-light as she pounded toward it—no surprises there, as was its absolute lack of movement as she skidded to a halt in front of it. Thankfully, it had a manual access panel on *this* side too—she clawed at the panel for a mindless second, then remembered her toolkit and wrenched it off her utility belt. After what felt like an eternity but couldn't have been more than a minute or two, she had the panel cover pried off.

Her fingers were still a few millimeters from the lever when a fat yellow spark jumped from it, snapping into her exposed skin—she shrieked, more from surprise than pain, and yanked her hand back. She started to reach for it again and thought better of it—the SeMI *had* to have done it, turned on some security protocol or something. That realization came simultaneously with *but my gauntlets are insulated!* and *Holy shit, I left my gauntlets AND MY SUIT HELMET back on the console*—

Carollene lurched back up to her feet and wheeled back around to face the console, just as the door at the far end of the fishbowl cycled open.

Time seemed to slow, freeze into a hideous tableau—Carollene, half-crouched on the balls of her feet, every muscle straining forward towards the helmet and gauntlets sitting in plain sight on top of the console; Sancia, motionless in the open doorway. Sancia, liberally blood-splattered—how much of it was hers, and how much...? Carollene's wide, staring eyes locked on Sancia's face, on the dull black orbs framed by long hair now stringy with drying blood. A shudder shook Sancia's metal frame, and for the first time since Carollene had seen her, her facial muscles moved—her mouth fell open, just a little. The klaxon shut off; in the dead silence that followed, Carollene could hear the faint wheeze of Sancia breathing. Another shudder jerked the metal frame, and Sancia's mouth opened wider. A low, croaking sound issued from her throat.

Carollene darted forward. A handful of bounding, giant steps brought her back to the console; she snatched up her helmet and gauntlets, then turned and pelted back to the entry door, fumbling the gauntlet onto her right hand. She dropped down to her knees and shoved her arm in the panel, her gloved fingers clamping down hard on the door lever. This time, the electrical surge didn't confine itself to a few puny sparks; the flare of power lit up the entire wall in front of her, scorched the fingertips off the gauntlets, and plunged straight into Carollene's all-too-conductive body. Carollene spasmed hard enough to rip her hand off the lever, eyes rolling back in her head, and thumped to the floor in an ugly, motionless heap.

HostName= FarHorizonRF01-SeMI-00
    HostID=c615d983-a399-44a0-8111-e906ae39c482
    DateTime=232112031600
    RunJobs: 2025/0008/COUNTER: PAUSED
Is she dead? Is she dead? Is she dead?
SANCIA INCONCLUSIVE
I told her to wait!—*she wasn't like* them, *she was trying to* help—
    >Power on: ROOMMONITOR ROAMING SENSOR 00/01/02/03/04
    ADHOCJOB03:   Remote   medical protocol self-check.
    2025/0009 ADHOCJOB03: OK

ADHOCJOB04:   Roaming   sensors online.

2025/0010 ADHOCJOB04: OK

PULSE 0. RESP 0/0. BP 80/45. CT 95C.

DBQUERY: 'electrical shock medical treatment':<'cardiopulmonary resuscitation'>

>Administrator\SANCIA: MOBILITY APPARATUS overclock 110/120/130

SANCIA   WARNING!   Health   monitor REDLINE SANCIA NOK SANCIA

I don't care! We have to get her to Medbay!

HostName= FarHorizonRF01(arch)_OstatnyRF01(online)-SeMI-00

HostID=c615d983-a399-44a0-8111-e906ae39c482

DateTime=232201251449

RunJobs: RESET/00000

The *Ostatny's* bridge was quiet, even peaceful—Carollene, sprawled out in the astrogator's console chair, eyed it all with a sense of astonishment mingled with satisfaction. She had done it, *really* done it. She thought she must have doubted herself, even doubted the entire proposition, more than she'd realized over the past several days of back-breaking labor. "I don't think I quite understood how *many* physical components you had, before this—you're sure we moved everything over here?" The bridge lights pulsed once. "And you're positive we got *all* the interfaces with the ship's own systems working?" The bridge lights pulsed twice, almost impishly; Carollene grinned in spite of herself. And her back, no matter how much it ached from all the lifting, carrying, endless hours of installing, was *not* broken at all—she twisted an arm around to touch the curve of her spine, gingerly. The shipsuit was warm and rough under her fingertips; she gave it a quick pinch, smiling bemusedly, then clutched at the console as the entire chair listed alarmingly to the left.

"The chair! It's broken." She wrinkled her forehead. "I think I did know that, actually." She reached for the astrogation console and tapped the screen. It lit up, but her expectant smile faded at the forest of yellow *Warning! Caution! ALERT!* messages abruptly crowding it. "Wow. That can't be good." Her fingers drifted lightly across the screen's surface. "You know I don't know anything about this. How to fix all this, I mean." She paused. "It wasn't our specialty. *Isn't* our specialty."

An icon bloomed on the screen, scarlet and blue with laurel leaves woven through the ornate, old-fashioned font: *Welcome to Far Horizon, paradigm-changing technology for future generations!* An image of a page shimmered into existence —*Specifications for the Moughton-Hesaki D-Class XPL Cargo Freighter*, read the header. The screen flicked to a second page, then a third, fourth, faster and faster until they were a whirling blur, dense with tables and schematics. "Oh, good, you found the ship drive manuals! At least it *has* manuals. I was worried about that. We didn't think much of the captain, you know. *I* didn't think much of him, either."

The console screen flickered; the schematics were replaced by thickly worded page with a small, bold header: *"Consciousness transference in vegetative patients with non-traumatic brain injury with real artificial intelligence: A bioelectrical and surgical approach."* Far Horizon Research Facility One.

Carollene looked sharply away. "It didn't really work out the way I hoped," she said softly into the *Ostatny's* wheezing silence. "I thought maybe—after we did it she would still be there with us, you and me, you know? *Really* with us, not just some memories." Grief pinched the skin between her brows. "Maybe we just weren't fast enough, maybe her heart was stopped too long—"

The screen blanked, leaving only the yellow error messages scrolling in a band across the bottom, then switched to a familiar, pearlescent gray, punctuated with plain black font: *SANCIA READY PRELAUNCH SEQUENCE?*

Carollene glanced down at her hands, lightly clasped together in her lap; after a second, they unclasped themselves and rose up to rest gingerly on the console's smooth, cold screen. "We've got this. We *do*." Her fingers trembled against the screen, then stilled. "We know what we're doing."

SANCIA OK, the screen announced firmly. *OK OK OK.*

"Yeah, I'm *OK OK*—but you know what? We'd better change that admin tag."

The screen flickered once. Then:

>username:Administrator\SANCIA
login:*************
>Login SUCCESSFUL
>ALTER   USER   'SANCIA'
withName='CAROLLENE JONAITIS'

"Right." Carollene sat up straighter. "*Now* it's time to go, huh?" She ran her hands through what was left of her hair, wincing as her fingers accidentally bumped into the still-healing scars ridging her scalp. "Okay, drives *on*—wow, they do sound terrible. We'll have to work on that. We'll have plenty of time to figure them out, though. After all, we're pretty good at making things work out in the end, aren't we?"

See Lisa Short's story "Far Horizon" online at Metaphorosis.
If you liked it, leave a comment. Authors love that!
Remember to subscribe to our e-mail updates so you'll know when new stories are posted.

About the story

This story was actually inspired by an open submissions call for another publication a few years ago—I didn't come anywhere near finishing the draft of the story I envisioned in time to submit it to them, though. I put away the thousand or so words I'd already generated, but the story idea did stay with me; I wanted to finish it! There's been a lot of hoopla around AI in recent times, and this story at least somewhat reflects my intermittent exasperation with the situation, specifically what "AI" means as envisioned by speculative fiction writers and IT professionals (both of which describe me) and what "AI" means as advertised by people trying to sell it to those who are neither. Basically, "AI" is not "intelligent" and is not even remotely close at present times to "intelligent..." (but then a little voice in the back of my head whispered, what if an "AI" could actually be integrated with something that was intelligent, genuinely intelligent? What would that look like?)

A question for the author

Q: Are titles easy or hard for you? Do you start with the title or the story?

A: It's funny because sometimes, the title of a story just comes to me—that is how the story itself comes to me, as a title! However, when this does not occur (which it doesn't the majority of the time), generating a title for a story is often a brutal slog. If I really, really just can't come up with anything by the time I've written the entire first draft—and I am usually trying to think of something the whole time I'm writing—I have a matrix I use, where I free-associate and write down absolutely any and every word that comes out of that brainstorming session that has anything at all to do with the story.

About the author

Lisa Short is a Texas-born, Kansas-bred, Maryland-resident writer of speculative fiction.

www.lisashortauthor.com;   @Lisa_K_Short   on X/Twitter, Instagram, and Threads; lisashortauthor.com on Bluesky

A word about Thomas Ha

We first published Thomas Ha with "Where the Old Neighbours Go" in September 2020, just four years ago. He followed up quickly with "A Compilation of Accounts Concerning the Distal Brook Flood" in April 2021 and "Orla, Always" in December of the same year.

Thomas' stories have quickly and deservedly drawn attention — winning and nominated for major awards, reprinted in *Year's Best* anthologies, singled out in industry roundups, etc. Thanks to fluid, literate prose and well developed characters, he's clearly an author whose impact will grow, and we're happy to have him in *Metaphorosis* again with his latest story, "The Fairgrounds"

The Fairgrounds

Thomas Ha

Young boys in love will do stupid and dangerous things.

Henry's grandmother had warned him of it, that night, when he was headed to the fairgrounds alone, now that he'd finally reached the age to attend unaccompanied. She had wrapped his olive green scarf around his neck and lowered his wool cap, and looked into his eyes to say that thing about boys in love because she seemed to sense why he was going and whom he was going for.

"So I'm not allowed?"

"What?"

"To the fairgrounds. You're not going to let me go?"

"I didn't say that," his grandmother answered. And she hesitated, as if she wanted to say something more, but wiped her hands on a dish towel and pursed her lips instead. "Just take care, Henry. That's all. Now go, before it gets too late."

And so, Henry left: first walking, then running out the back door. He scooped up his bike and hopped on and pedaled down the crooked and hilly street, squeezing his handlebars while the crisp not-quite-winter prickled his ungloved hands. His cheeks and his chest felt unusually warm. He was too excited to feel any tightness in his legs as he pedaled past the sheriff's station and the children's park and the Main Street shops.

Henry thought only of her as he rode to the fairgrounds. Seeing her, like a kind of apparition in the darkened sky, or in the branches of the maples along the houses —the girl who sat at the school desk just two seats in front of him, over by the window, with light glossing the river of dark hair that ran down her back.

Grete.

She had only joined Henry's class recently, in the early, leaf-laden days of

October. Her family had moved to the town from somewhere far, like Oregon, which to Henry was just a word, like Europe or Babylon. But those days since her arrival had been filled with a new kind of slow wonder for Henry and many quiet daydreams about the kind of person she might be. He had heard someone say she was Michael McCormick's cousin, or maybe related to the Changs who lived across the street from the library.

But he had never gotten close to asking about her. Every time she turned to pass papers back, he dared only look at her for a second, then down again at his desk before her eyes could ever meet his. It was just her name and its sound repeated in his thoughts, like some secret part of the Hail Mary that no one had taught him.

Grete.

The blurred glow of the fairground lights just beyond the town center rose as he pedaled uphill, pushing harder to meet the crest where laughter and music were beginning to grow louder. Henry dropped his bike next to a railing and fumbled with the chain. Unable to find his lock, he decided just to tie it and hastily hid the wrapped links under the body of the bike.

When Henry reached the entrance flags, he dug into his pockets and carefully unfolded the seventeen dollars he had saved from cleaning yards and moving Mr. O'Leary's garage boxes. The bills felt hot in his hand.

Grete.

The ticket-taker materialized next to the meter. Colors flashed and jarring music blared as his mustachioed face lit the air and crackled. "Welcome, welcome, to the fairgrounds, son. If you'd kindly scan your I.D. tag down at the screen and follow the prompts."

Henry swiped his wrist tag and fed four dollars into the machine for a child's ticket.

"Thanks, HENRY. Are your folks here with you, by any chance?"

"No, but...I'm—I'm old enough. Like my I.D. tag says. Twelve and a half."

"Ah. Yes, I can see your tag information here." The image of the ticket-taker blinked and crackled. "But unaccompanied minors can only stay until eight, which—well, that's coming up very soon. I'm not sure I should be letting you in, really, with how close the first closing is, but..."

Henry held his breath for just a moment, and then the face filled with light looked left and right and gave him a little smile.

"But okay, HENRY. You go on ahead. Just be quick, understand? You've got less than an hour before they have to escort you out. Go on. Go on." The ticket-taker winked.

"Thank you!" Henry said, in almost a shout, and hurried onto the grounds. His shoes squished almost immediately into wet mud matted with grass and hay, and every step grew slower as he trudged through, trying to get his bearings.

Teenage couples held hands and whispered the way young lovers did in the movies. Above, where the bright hanging bulbs bled light upward into the darkness, Henry saw the holographic projections of people riding one of the twisting glare-coasters. They were screaming and whooping from one of the tents below, where their bodies were strapped into rows of chairs with immersive goggles and sensor beads.

Near one of the booths, a girl younger than Henry was eating a giant blue synthesized cotton candy, ripping tufts away and stuffing her face while her parents took pictures of her. The three of them were dressed in down coats, nice ones, with no loose threads or missing buttons. Henry watched them, the way they talked and laughed, and he thought about buying one of those cotton candies, too, before remembering why he was here.

Are you going tonight, Henry? To the fairgrounds?

Henry had almost missed her question, that afternoon, when Grete had tapped his shoulder, right there, in a soft spot next to his collarbone. She had been out in the hallway, holding her books to her chest. And in the hours since, he imagined the moment again, and again, her in front of him, like that. Her eyes, big, and maybe only in his mind, with a hint of sadness in them.

My father, he won't let me go. But I hear it's fun. Is that true? That it's a lot of fun to go, when they pass through town in the fall?

Y-yes. It's...it's fantastic.

And that was it, really, all he had managed to say before she left, waving as she went off to find someone. It was probably no longer than half a minute, if even that. But that little tap on the shoulder, that question, was how the idea, small at first, had begun to grow—the idea Henry had, of showing Grete the fairgrounds, even if her father wouldn't allow her to go there herself.

He'd find a way to bring a piece of it for her, he thought. He was old enough now, knew enough now, to buy something like that. Maybe a toy or a streamer or something else. That could work. Something small and perfect that would impress her. That was the plan.

Are you going to the fairgrounds?
Yes. It's…it's fantastic.
Fantastic…

And there it was. Right where Henry had hoped. The virtual text crawled up and down the electronics of the tent fabric, the way that it had the year before, and the year before that, and the year before that:

THE INCOMPARABLE, INCORRIGIBLE, ILLIMITABLE
PROFESSOR DIEDERIK VON KEMPELEN
NUMINOUS MIRACLEMAKER AND
PHYSIKER EXTRAORDINAIRE

Henry knew that if he had any hope of bringing Grete something she would like, it would be here, with this man, the one everyone called Professor DVK.

The boy passed through the canvas threshold and into the little world of the Professor's curiosities. Much of it was unchanged since the last time Henry had been inside, as though the fair had never left town and the tent hadn't moved an inch. There was that strange and oily smell, like a doctor's office combined with the perfume shop his grandmother would visit. And on each side, a series of tables and shelves, displaying every manner of delights from faraway lands. A mummified hand with a bionic eye in its palm waved from its jar of preserving liquid. In a terrarium, a metallic snake slithered its segmented body over and around a gnarled branch. There were all kinds of unusual devices and containers cluttering the tabletops and crowded under chairs.

And, at the back of the tent, there he was: the man whose every thought and idea were manifested within the circumference of this little canopy— Professor DVK—sitting in the deepest meditative peace, so that he almost seemed to be asleep, with smoke rising from his pipe in concentrated, uniform puffs.

"Oh."

The Professor opened one eye slowly to look at Henry, then the other eye quickly. And there was a squeal from the microphone in his throat-box as the Professor jerked to his feet. The faintest hint of light surged through portions of his skin.

"Well, hello there! Yes. Hello there! Hello!" The Professor straightened and smoothed his jacket lapels. "Welcome, please. Yes. Come in, come in. Don't be shy, don't be shy. How may I help you this fine evening..." The boy's tag information flashed in his pupils briefly. "HENRY?"

"Hello, Professor," Henry began, aware of the fact that first closing was drawing in, and he looked here and there at the Professor's contraptions for something he might buy. "I'm so glad I made it, because I—I don't have much time. I was hoping to find something. Something nice. For a gift," Henry explained.

"Oh, a gift." The Professor's eyes flashed again, probably reviewing whatever information the fairgrounds had stored on Henry from previous visits or from publicly available data. "For your... GRANDMOTHER, perhaps?"

"What?" Henry's face went red. "No, for someone else. A friend."

"Ahh," Professor DVK stroked his beard. "A friend. I see. I see, HENRY. Well, there are many types of friends and many types of gifts. What type of person is this friend of yours? What do they like?"

"I'm not sure," the boy said, speaking the realization aloud.

"Well, what are their interests?"

"I'm not sure."

"What seems to excite them?"

"I'm...not sure."

"This is a most difficult task, then, for you, isn't it?" The Professor stood and paced around the inside of the tent. "Because, you know as well as I do—the act of giving a gift is about reception, how it is interpreted, what it signifies, not to you, but to them. And that's a near-impossible thing to know when you get right down to it. Not just in this instance, but in general. How well do we ever know anyone else, HENRY? How well do we know anyone? Not well at all! No, we do not."

Henry wasn't sure how to respond to the Professor, so he nodded along.

"Look, HENRY. You're a shining scion of the suburbs, practically full grown. So I think you are old enough to understand that I *could* string you along with something, if I really wanted—if I were the kind of man to do that sort of thing. I could offer you any of these trinkets or baubles or ingenious inventions and sell you some half-concocted story. Like, say, this neon spinning cyber-wheel: *forged with schematics from the ancient bricoleur-masters of the West*, I might tell you. Or this hanging chime: *designed using sonic sutras to find frequencies most pleasing to every individual!* But, listen, you would see through it, HENRY. And I'm *not* that sort of person, despite how I may appear and what they might be saying about me, out there. You'll get no silly stories, no misleading mumbo jumbo, no flim-flam from me!"

Henry did not know who or what the Professor was talking about, but he kept nodding, thinking only that he would have been perfectly happy with either the wheel or the chime the Professor had mentioned. The wheel or the chime would have made a perfectly good gift for Grete, he thought.

"You must understand, HENRY. As a gentleman of the Order of Perpetual Exchange, I couldn't possibly sully my reputation by giving you just any old novelty for whatever amount of petty cash you happened to bring. I take this completely, completely seriously, such that every customer's wish matters as if they were my own. HENRY. Ohhhh, dear boy. HENRY. How much money do you have on you, by the way?"

Henry held out what remained in his pockets, the thirteen dollars that were left after the entrance fee.

"Oh. Child." The Professor plucked each of the bills from Henry's hands and unfolded them on his desk. "I'm not even sure we have anything that would fit your humble means. But perhaps, that, in itself, is a blessing, because it rules out most of what I would probably have suggested. A blessing, yes."

Henry felt a little bit of a sinking feeling in his stomach upon hearing the Professor say this. And in his mind, that place where he saw Grete next to the classroom window, felt almost as if it was beginning to darken. That idea of her, that apparition, fading in and out of his mind, waning with the hope that he might have something to give her.

"But, wait!" The Professor slapped the table. "I do have something, HENRY. Yes! It might not be quite right, but it would fit matters like this, HENRY. Yes!" The man's excitement, his energy, filled Henry with a small burst of possibility, and like that, he could see Grete right there, by the window in his mind, again.

"What is it, Professor?"

"Come with me." The man laid a hand gently on Henry's shoulder and guided the boy over to one side of the tent, past several large cases and dummies dressed in sweeping robes and costumes, near a big shape that Henry initially thought to be furniture.

"Have you heard of the Kastenherz, HENRY?"

Henry had not, and he told the Professor so.

Professor DVK waved a hand at the large metal box, which was about the size of a wardrobe and covered in a series of tubes and blinking lights. "This here, HENRY, is the apex of artistry, distilled. Forward-looking fantasy fuel. In a word, the *future*.

"The Kastenherz is engineered to analyze your innermost thoughts. It reads your spirit, your essence, by divining it from the air, the ambience, like the most mystical of antennae. It takes the information, interpolates, collates, consecrates, and then *voila*: it re-imagines and gives you, not what you *think* you *want*, but what it *knows* you *need*, HENRY. And that's its true genius, my boy. Because needs are tricky. They're never what we suspect. The devil lives in expectation as easily as disappointment. None of us want 'happy', *per se*, not in the strictest sense. We want difficulty. Intrigue. Excitement. Triumph. The beauty of the Kastenherz is that it interprets that for you. A test run. Let's give it a test run. We won't count this one to start, understand? What's your friend's name?"

"Grete."

The Professor hurried to the side of the large machine and fiddled with a few buttons and sliders. "Yes. Yes. Yes," the man muttered. A wheel and series of cogs turned in one quadrant of the box, in another part, something like pistons moved up and down. Henry watched as pixels danced on a small screen, forming different shapes—a heart, a skull, a horse, and then a moon.

Professor DVK clapped and howled with an infectious enthusiasm, and then they watched a piece of paper emerge from a thin slat into a tray near the bottom of the box. The Professor snatched it and then handed it over to Henry with a cheerful smile. The paper read:

Come, you, 'cross the autumnal divide, sleeping and walking toward the sundered boars,
No one knows their origins, but you wonder how they all once sang,
And you reach for beautiful reliquaries beyond holy grasping delight,
While Arion watches and holds men to the river, filling their broken heads with dreams,
Oh, GRETA, you GRETA, know only what skies hold in our way of going,
Cross those divides, Margaret's Sundries, purchases 20% off on Sundays,
GRETA, sweet GRETA, if only there were other ways to know the mind except sleep,
Then, perhaps, we would know your peace, GRETA.

"What?" Henry stared.

Professor DVK's plastered smile did not budge.

"It's...Professor, I don't..."

"Know how to thank me? A beautiful poem for a beautiful girl. The Kastenherz knows, see? This is what you give a friend like yours."

"It's...I don't know what this means. And it's not her name."

"Her name?"

"It's wrong. Her name is Grete. G-R-E-T-E. It's an 'e' at the end."

"Well, you didn't specify, HENRY," he clucked his tongue. "And it's just a test, a warm-up, like I said. So don't worry yourself with details like an 'e' or an 'a.' Miracles come in miles, not in minutiae."

"I don't know what that means—"

They were interrupted, then, by a movement at the entrance. A little girl, the same little girl outside that Henry had seen eating synthesized cotton candy, had come bounding in with her father and mother, all well-dressed and clean and happy. Professor DVK's eyes were noticeably drawn to them as information, important-seeming information, flashed by in his pupils.

"Professor, I—"

"One moment, HENRY. I must see to these fine people for a minute or two."

"But Professor," Henry cried and grabbed his hand. "The first closing. They're going to make me leave the fairgrounds soon."

"HENRY." The Professor's smile was gone, and the excitement and mirth in his voice evaporated, as if it had never been there. And it was slight, but everything from his eyes to his posture hardened when he looked down. "There are rules. An order of priority. You know how these things work. So wait your turn, and, *after* I see to them, we will finish up with you. Understand?"

The Professor shook Henry off, picked up the corners of his mouth into a big smile, and then turned to face the incoming family with joyfully open arms and talk of the wonders he planned to show them in short order.

Henry, meanwhile, stared at the piece of paper from the machine. He couldn't bring himself to look at the Professor, or anyone. He couldn't even bring himself to think of the classroom window and Grete, for comfort. That proud feeling he'd imagined, that puff of power when he presented her with the perfect gift, shrank and shriveled. Foolish, stupid, useless, small. Henry's eyes began to feel wet, and despite his best efforts, it felt like he was going to cry.

"I'm sorry. He's an asshole."

A voice spoke, barely audible, while the Professor continued to laugh and shout with the father of the little family at the other side of the tent.

Henry did not know where the voice had come from, but he turned toward the machine. He couldn't explain it, but he was filled with the strangest certainty that there was something else in the machine, living there, and it was speaking to him now.

"Yes, Henry. That's right. I am in here," the voice said. *"And I'm sorry about the misspelling. The output, the specific words, that's his doing, not mine."*

"Oh..." Henry said quietly. "That's... that's okay."

"He's like this often, by the way, the Professor. Nice and inviting, until he's not."

"It's...fine," Henry replied, even if it didn't feel that way.

"Look, you have to go soon, right? Before first closing, you said?" the voice asked. *"Can you help me? Please? Can you get me out of this thing? Take me with you?"*

Henry felt a compulsion, a curious pull in his thoughts, drawing him closer to the machine where there was a small area of darkened glass. Something floated behind it.

"He won't let me go."

"Won't let you go?"

"My father. And I just want to get out, just for a little while. But you'll help me, won't you? Please. It would mean everything to me."

Something about the way the voice spoke seemed familiar to Henry, like someone he knew. He touched a small button next to the glass, and it slid open. There was something on an interior shelf, but nothing like anything he had ever seen before—like a large egg but made of flesh-colored clay.

The egg turned, and a mouth in its skin smiled at him.

"There's a way out the back," the egg said, its voice clear now that the glass was open. "Take me, and we'll get out of here! Quick!"

Henry looked at the Professor, who was still talking and laughing with the family. First closing was almost upon them, and Henry knew that Professor DVK wasn't going to help him. Not now. Henry had seen things like this before, when he was with his grandmother in town—the way people in the stores and the parks would talk to other kids with mothers and fathers and nice coats, the way their gaze always drifted around and away from him.

And something about knowing that the Professor was like them too made Henry's heart burn with a cold anger, something new he didn't recognize.

"Let's go," the egg said. "Not much time. Come on!"

Henry could almost hear his grandmother in his mind—a warning, not to do what he knew he was going to do—that moment when he snatched the egg and then walked out of the back exit, hurrying around a few more turns until he reached a gap in the shadows of the tents where no one seemed to be around.

He placed the thing, the egg from the Kastenherz, on the wet grass, and it shook. Something seemed to be happening within the little thing. An eye swam next to another above the mouth, then came the lump of a nose, then more solid parts, like the clay that made up its shell was growing and expanding. After a few moments and a strange popping noise, Henry recognized a face formed from what used to be the egg, a face he had seen many times in his thoughts.

Grete.

The egg looked like the girl from Henry's class now.

Or, it looked like Grete's head, at least, with long hair spilling out on the grass, except instead of a glossy black, the hair was a soft white—like January frost.

"Thank you, Henry," the head that looked like Grete's said. "Could you pick me up?"

"What?"

"It's okay. Pick me up. We have to keep moving."

Henry lifted the head, then looked around worriedly—but none of the people over by the walkways seemed to be paying attention to him at all, perhaps distracted by more interesting and fantastical things in the main grounds. He thought to remove his olive green scarf, and carefully wrapped the head in it, leaving enough room for the head to breathe. And then he went backwards slowly, behind the tents, where rays of light from the main areas barely reached.

"What a relief," the head that looked like Grete with white hair smiled. "He never lets me stroll around like this, out here, you know. Forever. It really feels like forever, since I've been out of the box. Thank you."

"You're...you're welcome," the boy whispered, finding it odd to be looking at the face he'd imagined for so long, resting now in his arms. He was stunned by it, this thing from the Kastenherz, whatever it was, and how easily it seemed to change its form.

"And don't worry, Henry. I'm going to help you too."

"With Grete, you mean?"

"Keep going. That way."

Henry realized he was headed to parts of the fairgrounds he didn't usually go to. From between the tents he could see dozens of fairgoers gathered together, talking very loudly, some holding cups and others of them dancing. He'd heard of this place set aside for the older fairgoers, the social square.

Many of the people there were wearing holographic masks, hiding themselves with strangely lit disguises. There were a few who looked like they had giant bug heads, with clicking mandibles that dripped when they spoke. An older boy, much older, maybe fifteen or sixteen, turned the collar of his mask on and flipped through the presets until he'd made his head into a 20th century automobile. Cat people, bird faces, cartoon eyeballs were making noise, a kind of charged, excitable discussion like at a party.

And in the distance, by a bent oak, Henry recognized Father Joyce from the school chapel by his clergy shirt. He seemed to be dancing with a tall, very tall, maybe genetically enhanced person. And this person was wearing a mask of some kind of beast with curved horns, giggling and squeezing at Father Joyce's back.

For a short time, Henry tried to imagine Grete there too. He tried to picture how the two of them might wander out into that crowded area under the blaring trumpet music. How they would try on masks or dance or talk like the older kids and grownups were doing over there. But he couldn't quite see it, and the air felt too hot and noisy.

Something about those people and what they were doing made him uncomfortable, though he couldn't say exactly why.

"You can feel it," the head wrapped in Henry's arms said. "The emptiness in them. That doesn't go away. It just builds, you know."

"Oh."

He had heard many stories about the social square over the years, but this was all very different from what he had thought it would be.

So Henry kept moving, further away from the music, deciding he didn't want to see much more of this part of the fair. He wanted to know where they were going, but he sensed that the head would lead them and that he would know soon enough.

Under the walkway lights in the distance, Henry watched men made of stained glass performing for a small crowd. They banged against one another in mock battle. Again, again, again, until one of them shattered and the people clapped.

"We're almost there, Henry."

"And we'll find something there? A gift?"

"Not exactly," the head smiled. "When I read you from inside the Kastenherz, do you know what I saw, Henry?"

"What?"

Grete.

Henry was embarrassed, trying not to think of the image he'd been holding onto, of the girl by the classroom window, because he knew the head could probably see it too, with whatever talents it used to read his mind in the Professor's tent.

"Yes," the head laughed. "That was part of it. That girl was part of what I saw. But, what you wanted, it wasn't really about her under the surface. Like you told the Professor, you don't know her. Her interests. Her likes. No, Henry. What you want is something else."

"What's that?"

The head didn't answer. "We're here."

The sound of the fairgrounds seemed muffled and small. They were by a large black tent at the end of the lot, surrounded by darkness, crates, and trash. The mud here felt thicker, like pitch oozing from the edges of the black canvas. And everything smelled ripe and heavy— nothing like the candied air and popcorn where the crowds were.

"We're here to pay our respects. Come on."

Henry didn't know what that meant, but again, he felt that feeling he had at the Professor's place, a nudging in his thoughts, like the head that looked like Grete was prodding him. He followed the prodding, into the musty dark of wherever this was.

"Everything in the fairgrounds runs on flash," the head told Henry. "And my father likes it—to pretend that it's all modern miracles and machines. He hides the messy things from before, like me and others. He doesn't want people to know how old it all is, I suspect. And so he chases that bright flame of youth that's always just around the corner. The trends, the fashions. Desires and tastes. Always flickering, always changing, depending on the moment.

"Before the holographic, there was cybernetic, before cybernetic, mechanical, before mechanical, there was us."

As his eyes adjusted, Henry realized there were solid metal bars not so far to his left, and something long and scaly shifted behind them. To his right, another set of metal bars, and behind them, three golden eyes looked out at him. He continued forward, trying not to get too close to any one of what he assumed were cages, unsure what kinds of animals were moving about within.

Until eventually, they reached a large, dimly lit cage in the center of the tent.

A very big creature, with its back to them, slowly turned.

And at first, Henry thought it was a man he was looking at.

There were muscles and shadow that looked like a torso and long forearms extending into massive hands. But instead of a face staring back at Henry, it was the maned head, long muzzle, and wet nostrils of a horse. For a brief second, Henry thought that this was a person with a holographic mask, like the people in the social square, but there were no streaks of light, no glare, no trickery of that kind. This horse-headed man was nothing like Henry had ever seen or heard or read about, and a part of him was certain that this thing, and maybe all the things within the black tent, were not creatures he would find anywhere else.

"Kneel," the head that looked like Grete whispered.

So Henry did.

The horse-man leaned into a small patch of light from a hanging bulb, its black eyes drinking in everything in that tent, including the boy and the small head he carried. Henry felt that the other animals in the shadows of the tent were all watching carefully.

"He's the oldest of us, the strongest, but also the tiredest," the head smiled.

"He doesn't like being cooped up back here in this tent. Hasn't for a long time. Like me, in the box, I've felt it. So, he and I, we share a certain kind of understanding, I think."

There was a chill in the air. Henry heard sounds that weren't exactly sounds. Echoes he thought might be of the thing that looked like Grete, talking somehow to the horse-man, without words. The horse-man breathed heavily through its mouth, and those eyes, like pools of reflective oil, studied them for a while.

"Yes," the head that looked like Grete said. "No. Yes. I promise."

The horse-man's face loomed above Henry, silent.

"Yes."

The horse-man shifted, just slightly, but it was enough that Henry began shaking involuntarily. The creature did not lunge, only moved its heavy body closer to the bars. Then the horse-man extended a large wrinkled hand with its palm upward.

"Go on," the head that looked like Grete said. "Give me to him, Henry. It's okay."

The boy was afraid, but he was more afraid of disobeying. He unwrapped his scarf and raised the head, placing it into the huge palm in front of him, and the frosty hair streamed down between the creature's callused fingers.

The head that looked like Grete started quivering, much like it had when it changed its shape before, outside the tents. The edges of the head puffed, expanded, and the skin of Grete's face seemed to stretch and latch onto the horse-man's giant hand. The fleshy parts kept growing, seeming to swallow up the large fingers and palm.

"Close your eyes, Henry," the head said.

And Henry closed his eyes.

Grete, he said to himself.

Grete.

Grete.

He thought of the window. Streaming light. Wooden desks. Dark hair. He imagined her two seats in front of him, looking out, looking back. A smile. He tried to ignore the sounds of loud and rapid breathing coming from the cage ahead. He tried to ignore the strange roars, the chattering, the screeches starting to rise from other cages in other parts of the tent too, crescendoing.

Grete.

Grete.

Grete.

That secret part of the Hail Mary he recited to drown out the noise, growing louder and more intense, like it was all whirling around his head.

Grete.

Grete.

Grete.

Again and again and again and again and...then.

Everything stopped.

There was only the weight of silence and stillness, and a small, familiar voice.

"Okay, Henry. You can look."

Henry didn't want to, and he waited. But eventually, he did open his eyes. When he did, he saw that the cage was empty. The horse-man, whatever it was, or whatever it had been, had vanished. And instead, in front of the cage, next to him, she stood.

The thing, so much like Grete.

Her hair, soft and bright, like the moon. A neck, shoulders, arms, legs, and wearing a white dress like most girls wore to church.

"All done," the girl said, as lumps of skin seemed to rise and sink near her throat. There was some kind of movement there, inside of her, that made Henry look away. He tried to peer into the shadows, toward the other darker edges of the black tent, and he realized the other cages, what he could make of them, seemed to be empty too.

"Did you...hurt them?" he finally asked.

Not-Grete shook her head.

"Of course not. I'm helping them, like you helped me. Just in a different sort of way."

Henry did not know what that meant, or what had happened, but he was too afraid to ask and too scared to look around any further.

"Come on." Not-Grete laughed and she reached out and held Henry's hand. She was warm, small, and gentle. He focused intently on her hand. "Let's go."

He followed her, out of the black tent, out under the stars. She interlaced her fingers with his and led him back toward the noise and the movement and the people walking. The laughter and the lights out here felt strange now to Henry, having seen what was back there, in the dark. But he kept on walking.

A loud chime rang over the fairgrounds to announce the first closing. A number of children and families were going in a slow throng toward the entrance flags together. Not-Grete squeezed Henry's hand and leaned on him, and he felt relaxed, fuzzy, like he was in some kind of dream.

The two of them walked between those others, shuffling, and Henry saw Professor DVK, far off, standing in front of his tent, scanning the grounds like he was looking for something. The Professor's eyes reached them, and he froze, his body perfectly still.

The Professor's face blanched, and something flashed in his pupils as he stood there. Henry wasn't sure, but he thought the Professor recognized something in Not-Grete, something that made him too terrified to say or do anything as they walked away. The Professor seemed so small to Henry then —just a withered version of the man in the tent—smaller and smaller in the distance, until they left him behind completely.

When they reached the outside of the entrance, Not-Grete took Henry over to his bike, still unchained, and propped it up for him. She looked into his eyes and smiled sweetly.

"Thank you, Henry. For tonight. We won't forget this, you know," she whispered, and, for a brief moment, Henry thought he heard other voices in the wind that softened and were swallowed by the crinkling of leaves. "Anytime you need us, anytime at all. We will be there for you. Just think it, and we will come. We mean it. We promise."

Henry stuttered, unsure of his words. He looked at her face, so much like Grete, but so clearly something else, leaning forward to press her lips gently against his cheek. And he felt his face burn.

Then she turned, like she was tracking the shapes of the people nearby—and there was the family from the Professor's tent earlier, nice and clean, the father, the mother, and the little girl. And Not-Grete had a strange expression on her face as she followed them with her eyes, which appeared darker than before. Henry didn't like that look in her for some reason.

"Goodnight," she said.

"Goodnight."

"Think about what we said, Henry. About what you wanted. What you really wanted, when you were looking for that gift of yours." She smiled. "You already got it, you know."

Henry didn't understand, but before he could ask her, Not-Grete walked away, like an animal slinking into the night. He wondered if she meant it, what she had said, about being there when he needed her, always there, somewhere. And part of him felt happy about that, but another part, a smaller part of him, felt unusually cold.

Henry trudged away from the fairgrounds—down the hill and up another, pulling his bike in a daze. When he returned, everything was bright and warm inside his grandmother's house. He felt too tired to talk, but he went to the kitchen where his grandmother was waiting. She had prepared a bowl of rice soup and watched as he shed his cap and scarf and sat silently, eating. She somehow seemed to know that he didn't want to say much, and so she didn't pry or ask how things went.

After he'd finished and gotten ready for bed, his grandmother was there to press his blankets over him and brush the hair from his eyes, talking to him as she often did, while he got sleepier and sleepier.

"The fairgrounds are strange," he heard his grandmother say. "Like everything out there. Heavy, their strangeness."

"Yes…" Henry said softly.

"There's no hiding that from you," his grandmother said. "The more you go out, the more you'll see. Not just in the fairgrounds. But everywhere else too. The fairgrounds are just a concentrated piece of it, a symbol, of whatever else there is out there."

"Yes…" he agreed.

"And it's not always good, not always bad. It's just there, everywhere, and you find it and make things of it as you go on in life. We all have to."

"Yes…" he said.

"You have to be careful with what you make of it. Promise me you'll be careful. Because I can't do it for you." Henry's grandmother searched his eyes, like she had some notion of what he'd been through, but not enough to ask him in detail. And Henry had the feeling that this might be the way it would be between them, not just for this, but other things to come.

"I promise," he said.

"You've had a day, I can see. So I'll let you rest. Goodnight, Henry. Goodnight. I love you very much, little one."

"I love you too."

The room went dark, and Henry stared drowsily at the ceiling. Somewhere in his mind, he felt the faintest glimmers of light and the softest sounds of distant music, drifting over.

He thought again about what his grandmother had said, about the fairgrounds as a kind of symbol—the strangeness it contained. The exciting, the frightening. The heartbreaking and the fun. And he imagined, beyond the house, the fairgrounds, and even the town, more bright and empty things he might one day find. Soft and precious things too. And a dull and ever-present ache that joined everything together.

These hazy thoughts filled him with a distant ease, but there was also, underneath it, a quiet sense that something terrible had happened tonight. Something important that he might have had a part in, but did not fully understand.

Not-Grete had said he had gotten what he'd wished for, and, the more he thought about that too, and about Grete, the more part of him realized it had never really been a girl, or a gift for her, that he had yearned for, not really. He would see her again, on Monday. And the day after—

there, in the classroom. And maybe they would talk more, but, more likely, they wouldn't. His young mind would drift wherever it would drift next, and his brittle sense of her would fall away like the crackling leaves before the season's end.

Like the fairgrounds, Henry thought, the longing he thought he felt might have really been a piece of something else. Of knowing things, and of growing older, and of becoming more like all the others.

Of growing up.

Henry dropped further into the fullness of sleep, and as he did, he tried to imagine the familiar window again, and the desk near it where the light fell. He tried to see the girl that sat there, the way he had before, but the memory of her already felt insubstantial, like smoke.

Grete, he thought.

Grete, he prayed.

Grete, he dreamed.

Less a boy, less a child, he grasped for it, the feeling that had been in him before.

Grete.

But he wasn't sure he would ever find that same feeling again.

See Thomas Ha's story "The Fairgrounds"
online at Metaphorosis.
If you liked it, leave a comment. Authors love
that!
Remember to subscribe to our e-mail updates so
you'll know when new stories are posted.

About the story

This story was heavily inspired by James Joyce's "Araby". A young boy goes to a bazaar to impress a crush and leaves with new, mixed feelings about the world and his place in it. When I read it when I was younger, there was just something very powerful and palpable about that kind of "first crush" feeling and the rollercoaster that entailed. I wanted to take that basic core and add to it, complicate it. This world also has strains of Bradbury's dark carnival stories, like "Something Wicked This Way Comes", among others, with some sci-fi and weird fiction elements layered in too. And lastly, I thought this mirrored my very first story in Metaphorosis, "Where the Old Neighbors Go". Both are sort of classic speculative fiction that's not entirely devoid of hope, but not entirely glossy and romantic either. It's dark and it's strange, there's pain, and there's some love and familial affection in it too. It's the kind of story I like and like to share, I guess.

A question for the author

Q: Are you a Luddite? Or do you have the latest and greatest technology?

A: Boy, that's a topical question! I know Luddites are being heavily debated again lately, especially their opposition to the ways in which technology may be misused to exploit labor (rather than being opposed to just the tech itself). I guess my answer is that I'm always wary of new technology, particularly when it extracts value and doesn't necessarily create anything of value in return. I'm slow to trust new developments as a general matter, though, so that probably isn't limited to tech!

About the author

Thomas Ha is a former attorney turned stay-at-home father who enjoys writing speculative fiction during the rare moments when all of his kids are napping at the same time. Thomas grew up in Honolulu and, after a decade plus of living in the northeast, now resides in Los Angeles.

thomashawrites.com, @thomasha.bsky.social

A word about Philip McCulloch-Downs

Philip is a vegan artist based in Somerset in the UK. He has spent all his adult life exploring and refining his creative skills and has learned how to process the varied experiences of everyday life through his art, video-making, novels and poetry.

Since 2014 his artwork has entered the world of veganism and animal rights. His series of uncompromising paintings 'Moving Pictures' attempt to dignify the creatures we abuse and to bear witness to their suffering by recording it with accuracy, empathy and compassion. He also produces vibrantly coloured and highly detailed pieces in ink and acrylic paint that celebrate the beauty and majesty of free-living wildlife.

He has exhibited his art prints at *Vegfests* and vegan events all over the world, including the *International Animal Rights Conference* in Luxembourg. In 2020, he and fellow artist/activist Helen Barker created the online gallery "Agitate Art" on Youtube, as a showcase for all forms of 'Protest Art'.

www.philipdownsart.co.uk
instagram.com/vegan_artivist

Copyright

Title information

Metaphorosis Jul-Sep 2024

ISSN: 2573-136X (online)
ISBN: 978-1-64076-282-4 (e-book)
ISBN: 978-1-64076-283-1 (paperback)

Publisher

Metaphorosis Magazine is an imprint of
Metaphorosis Publishing
Neskowin, OR, USA

www.metaphorosis.com

"Metaphorosis" is a registered trademark.

Discounts available

Substantial discounts are available for educational institutions, including writing workshops. Discounts are also available for quantity purchases. For details, contact Metaphorosis at metaphorosis.com/about

Metaphorosis Publishing

Metaphorosis offers beautifully written science fiction and fantasy. Our imprints include:

Metaphorosis Magazine
Plant Based Press
Verdage
Vestige
Joyful Heave

You can also find us:
@metaphorosis.bsky.social (Bluesky)
@Metaphorosis@writing.exchange (Mastodon)
www.facebook.com/metaphorosis

Help keep Metaphorosis running by supporting us at
Patreon.com/metaphorosis

See more about some of our books on the following pages.

Plant Based Press

plant
based
press

Vegan-friendly science fiction and fantasy,
including anthologies of the year's best
SFF stories, from 2016-2020.

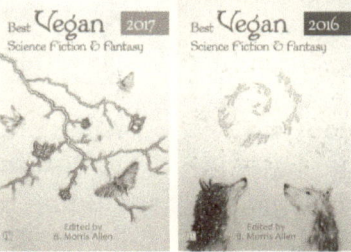

Chambers of the Heart

speculative stories
by
B. Morris Allen

A heart that's a building, a dog that's a program, a woman sinking irretrievably — stories about love, loss, and motion.

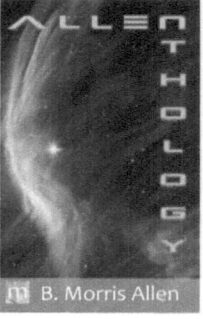

Susurrus

A darkly romantic story of magic, love, and suffering.

Allenthology: Volume I

Including three full collections of SFF stories.

Verdage

Science fiction and fantasy books for writers — full of great stories, often with an additional focus on the craft of speculative fiction writing.

Reading 5X5 x3

Changes

How do stories move from 'maybe' to published?

Here are 15 case studies of stories published in *Metaphorosis* magazine.

Reading 5X5 x2

Duets

How do authors' voices change when they collaborate?

A round-robin of five talented science fiction and fantasy authors collaborating with each other and writing solo.

Including stories by Evan Marcroft, David Gallay, J. Tynan Burke, L'Erin Ogle, and Douglas Anstruther.

Score

an SFF symphony

An anthology with an emotional score from the heights of joy to the depths of despair – but always with a little hope shining through.

Reading 5X5

Five stories, five times

See how different writers take on the same material.

Reading 5X5

Writers' Edition

Two extra stories, the story seed, and authors' notes on writing.

Vestige

Novelettes, novellas, and novels by Metaphorosis authors.

The Nocturnals
Mariah Montoya

Night is Dangerous. Day is deadly.

Where day and night last thirty years, humans move constantly stay ahead of the night and cruel Nocturnals that call it home. But a boy is lost out there.

Joyful Heave

Science fiction and fantasy anthologies with innovative and unusual themes.

Museum Piece
an unusual collection

A gallery of the strange and outrageous

Step right up and enter a world of wonder and oddities! These museums are not your typical tourist traps. From the Museum of Lost Dreams to the Suicide Museum, each exhibit will take you on a journey you won't soon forget.